To Pauline

Wishing you many
hours of relaxing
reading. I hope
you enjoy reading
this, my first
novel.

with love

Linda x

Memories Are
Made of Love

Linda Dowsett

Linda Dowsett

November 2009

authorHOUSE®

AuthorHouse™ UK Ltd.
500 Avebury Boulevard
Central Milton Keynes, MK9 2BE
www.authorhouse.co.uk
Phone: 08001974150

First published by AuthorHouse 10/26/2009

ISBN: 978-1-4490-0124-7 (sc)

This book is printed on acid-free paper.

LINDA DOWSETT was born in Bath but now lives with her husband of almost forty years in Southwick, Wiltshire. They have four children plus one adopted and between them and their partners they have produced 18 grand-children .

Linda only started reading romantic novels when she retired in 2006 and she became absolutely hooked .

Linda has been writing poetry for many years and has had poetry published under her pen name of Christine Linden . She has now turned her hand to romantic novels . She loves writing them and cannot believe that one can become so involved with the characters of the heroes and heroines and also the plots of the stories . They just come alive and seem so real in one's mind . She hopes that you enjoy reading them as much as she has enjoyed writing them .

When Linda is not writing she enjoys cooking, sewing, line dancing and appearing in pantomime at the local Southwick Entertainers Group

This book is for Win and Bob Coward who were
my friends for over 15 years and on whom the
characters of Harry and Sarah are based
With thanks to Anne-Marie Hunt .
Also to my three sons who taught
me how to use a computer
and to my dear friends Mary and
Eileen who proof read for me
Many thanks to Josh Heydon for his valuable assistance

Memories are made of love is a very tender love story.

Chapter 1.

"PHEW! That was close". Vicky gasped as she sat in the lounge of the boat struggling to get her breath back .She had only just made it in time to catch the ferry . She had left home just after 10 o'clock and thought she had allowed enough time to get to the terminal to catch the boat scheduled to leave at noon , but she hadn't bargained for so many hold-ups . She also hadn't thought about all the weekend shoppers or all of the other travellers going on holiday so she was just glad she had eventually made it in time , perhaps she could relax a little now.

She had decided to take two weeks holiday and thought that if she went to the Isle of Wight she would at least feel that she had 'got away from it all' with the stretch of water between her and the mainland .

She suddenly remembered that today was her niece Evie's 4th birthday and although she'd sent a card earlier in the week she thought it might be a nice idea to telephone Evie from the boat .She sat comfortably back in her seat and dialled . The phone rang and her sister-in-law Sally answered . "Could I speak to Evie please?".

Sally knew immediately who it was "Quick Evie , it's Auntie Vicky on the phone for you". When Evie answered Vicky sang her best rendition of 'Happy Birthday' much to the amusement of all the other passengers around her . Evie was thrilled and doubly pleased when Vicky told her she was phoning from a big ship . They chatted for a few moments then Vicky told Evie she hoped she would have a super day and that she would see her in a few weeks . They then said goodbye and Vicky hung up .

She was rather thirsty by now so she decided to get a drink . The boat had a snack bar and a good coffee shop so she went there to buy a take-away cappuccino . As the weather was bright and sunny she opted to take her coffee up top onto the deck . Although it was quite warm it was still very breezy but as she stood by the railings she felt really quite invigorated as the wind blew the cobwebs out of her naturally unruly curls .

She then took a seat on the deck and realised how much she had been looking forward to this break . She had booked two weeks in a small apartment in one of the double fronted Victorian houses right on the promenade in Sandown .Oh well better this holiday than none at all , she thought ruefully.

She had been working quite hard lately . She ran a Fancy Dress Hire business which was very interesting but also seasonal .She was always busy on Valentines Day, Halloween, Christmas and New year hiring out costumes and she also made numerous outfits for the pantomime season . It ticked over quite nicely and she loved meeting all the different kinds of people and helping them to live out their fantasies at a party . Couples loving the thought of being Anthony and Cleopatra , dressed in flowing white robes and gold costume jewellery or maybe Cinderella and Prince Charming with the allure of the Regency period of dress .Others wanting to be Peter Pan , Captain Hook , swash-buckling pirates or Tinkerbell . She had over seven hundred costumes which were a lot to look after with all the washing and ironing after each hire. She had just finished all the work after a very successful music festival and as she wasn't too busy in the Spring she'd decided she deserved a break .The weather was usually very pleasant in May so she thought it would be a good time to go on holiday. Vicky had recently decided that she might sell her business and try something new , but as yet hadn't decided what to do next . Maybe on this holiday she'd have time to think about it .She was anticipating hours of sunbathing on the beach plus a few sight-seeing trips to other parts of the island . She'd had her little car for twelve years now , it was a VW Polo and it had never let her down . Don't speak too soon , she thought , but it had served her well on her travels .

Over halfway across to their destination the ferry was just passing a large new cruise liner. Oh , to be sailing away to some exotic location for a few weeks and living in luxury on a ship like that , she thought as she looked enviously at the passengers she could see on the decks .Well I can dream can't I , she mused , as she leaned back in the chair and closed her eyes for a moment . In her minds eye she saw herself walking hand in hand with a faceless stranger on a sun kissed tropical island beach . In the distance exotic dancers were moving seductively to the rhythm of the drums sounding through the trees .

As they walked near the clear blue water Vicky could feel the soft warm sand under her feet .The stranger then led her to a secluded part of the beach and they laid down where unseen by others he drew her seductively into his arms and was just about to lower his lips to hers when she heard a voice come over a loud speaker "Ladies and gentlemen would you please return to your vehicles as we are nearing our destination". Vicky was disappointedly brought back to the present thinking that she very much doubted anything exciting like that would ever happen to her . Well she had better go back to her car , how quickly that hour had flown , she thought .

Soon she had left the terminal and was making her way south . She knew the way to Sandown and also that there was a supermarket on the way . She'd stop to fill up her petrol tank and stock up with all the groceries etc: that she would need for the first week at least .

After a gruelling hours shopping she thought it might be a good idea to have a refreshing cup of coffee so she put her shopping in the boot of the car and walked back to the supermarket restaurant . She bought the drink and as she was feeling a little peckish decided to buy a Kit-Kat chocolate bar .The place was pretty crowded as it was Saturday but she saw a small table at the far end . She started towards it but by the time she reached it a gentleman had sat down in one of the two chairs . Oh , drat ,she thought . Anyway she asked him if he minded her sharing his table .

"Not at all" he said with a breathtaking smile that almost took her breath away .

She looked at him and thought he was quite the most handsome man she had seen in ages. Wow , what a first impression she thought . He had raven black curly hair with short side-burns , stunning brown eyes and lips to die for . As she settled herself down she noticed he was wearing a very expensive , but modern , leather jacket . Under that he wore a crew neck sweater . As she came out of yet another day-dream she was thinking how exquisite he looked . She sipped her coffee and as it was a little hot she decided to eat her chocolate bar . She picked it up from the table , opened it and broke one of the fingers off and as she started to eat it she was amazed to see the man pick it up and break a finger off for himself . She immediately picked it up and broke the third finger off and ate it and he copied her with the last finger . Vicky was pretty angry by now and as he had a large cream doughnut on a plate in front of him, she leaned over , picked it up and took a big squidgy bite out of it and put it back on the plate . She then picked up her bag and stormed out "What a cheek", she mumbled to herself and she was quite sure she heard him chuckle as she walked away . As she reached the car park she was rummaging through her bag to find her car keys . The keys were right at the bottom and as she looked into her bag to her absolute astonishment she found the chocolate bar she had bought was still in her bag . "Oh my God!" she said aloud "I was eating his chocolate bar". She had never felt so embarrassed in her whole life . Well that's a good start to my holiday , she thought , but she couldn't bring herself to go back and apologise to him .

She drove to Sandown running through what had happened in her mind and then decided not to dwell on it , she would probably never see him again and wouldn't recognise him if she did .

Once she had arrived at the digs that she had booked for the next fortnight she felt a little more relaxed .

Before she unloaded the car she went to the side of the house where several little secure key boxes were situated on the wall . She tapped the code , which she had been given on her confirmation letter , into her designated box and retrieved the keys to the front door of the house and also the apartment .

She brought just her handbag and case from the car for the moment , let herself in and trudged up to the first floor . Her apartment was Number Four and when she had let herself in and put her case down in the small hallway she quickly glanced around and saw that the large bay window in the lounge and the small one in the kitchenette were facing the sea and she was really pleased about that . Although Vicky was a little daunted by the sea , as she was not a confident swimmer ,she still loved to watch the rolling waves and listen to them crashing onto the shore . She also loved to hear the sound of the seagulls and to see them soaring above the surf . She went back outside to her car and brought in the rest of her bags and her shopping .

It only took an hour to put away the shopping and unpack her case . She then made herself a cup of tea and sat down on the settee in the lounge and put her feet up . "Two weeks of peace and quiet and I'll go home fresh as a daisy" she said aloud .

She thought the lounge looked quite roomy as she looked around . It was brightly decorated in lilac pink with burgundy curtains in the bay window and matching carpet on the floor. There was a small dusky pink cottage suite situated almost centrally facing the fireplace , and in one corner there was a dining table and four chairs . The television was on a mahogany unit in the corner , although Vicky had decided before she came that she wouldn't be watching any television this next fortnight . What was the point of trying to get away from it all and then watching the news and feeling completely depressed about everything that was going wrong in the world .

Vicky's thoughts went back to the bedroom , she really liked that as well . As she had been putting her clothes away she had thought how spring-like it felt . The primrose yellow walls with a floral patterned frieze around the centre , pretty floral curtains with a matching bedspread and a pale green carpet . The kitchen was very basic but it had everything she needed .Yes , this will suit me fine ,she mused , I'll be quite happy here for a while .

After she had finished her drink she decided to have a shower before she prepared herself something to eat . The shower freshened her up nicely and she just popped on some slacks and a polo-neck sweater . Although May wasn't a cold month it did feel a little nippy in the early evening . She went to the kitchen and cooked herself a little snack , thinking that cheese on toast and a yoghurt would do for this evening . She sat down at the little table and actually felt quite lonely . She had left her little pet bird , Snowy , with her brother Jack and suddenly she realised that although he was only small he was her constant companion at home .He always chirped merrily and talked to her , flew on her shoulder as she ate her meals and now here on her own was when she missed him the most .

She finished her snack , popped through to the kitchen and washed the few dishes and then returned to the lounge to sit down again . She was determined not to watch any television so she decided she would go for a walk along the promenade . It was still quite early and she thought it would do her good before she went to bed . She had brought a long coat with her in case it got chilly or it rained . It was neither of these at the moment but she put it on anyway. She then locked the door of the apartment and made her way down to the front door of the house. As soon as she open the door she felt the cool breeze from the sea on her face , it was so invigorating the she stayed there for a few moments and soaked up the atmosphere.

As she walked along the sea front towards the pier she stopped , sat on the sea wall and closed her eyes and just listened to the sound of the roaring waves coming in , crashing onto the sand . Absolute bliss, she thought breathing in the sea air again and she knew she would sleep well tonight .

Next day was Sunday . What shall I do today , she thought as she stretched herself after having a really restful night . Looking at the alarm clock she'd brought with her she saw it was past 10 o'clock . Goodness she'd never had such a lie-in for ages .Oh! this is the life , she told herself as she went to have a quick shower and wash her hair . The shower room was very small with just the shower , a sink and toilet but it was quite adequate for her . When she'd finished she wrapped herself in a lovely large soft warm bath towel then went into the bedroom to dry her hair . Vicky had long dark mahogany curls which could be a little unmanageable at times . So while she decided whether to put it up or not she went over to the wardrobe to decide what she should wear . She chose a sunshine yellow skirt and a short sleeved white blouse and thought her white sling-back sandals would be suitably comfortable to walk in if she was going sight-seeing today . She had looked out of the window as she opened the curtains in the bedroom when she'd got up and the weather had looked very warm and pleasant .

Right , the hair , should she tie it back , no this week she wanted to feel free and letting her hair down was a statement to the way she felt.

When she had finished dressing she walked through to the kitchen and poured herself some orange juice , then made some scrambled egg on toast and a cup of coffee .

Today she decided she would go to Shanklin , to the olde village which was very romantic and rustic . Little did she know that today was going to change her life forever .

Vicky arrived in Shanklin and parked her car . She thought that maybe four hours would be ample in the car park and went across to the machine to fetch the ticket .

She thought it might be nice to take a few souvenirs home so she made her way to the gift shop . Browsing through she caught sight of a stand with small fridge magnets attached and after perusing quite a few her eyes fell on one that was particularly poignant . It said

A life time isn't long enough
for me to share with you
The dreams we dream together
hoping they'll all come true ,
Forever is too short a time and
all eternity can't see
The very special happiness that
you always give to me '

Oh , thought Vicky . to love a person that much to have written that about them must be so special , and she wondered if she would ever find someone who would feel that way about her .

Vicky had had quite a few boyfriends . She had courted one of them for several years and their relationship had seemed very special at the time . Her first love , as she thought , was Douglas . She had met him at University . They had hung out with a group that went everywhere together . He was very good-looking with blond hair and blue eyes , which she loved . At the time she thought he really loved her and that they would be together forever and she had no qualms surrendering her virginity to him . But as with most university romances it was not to be , and they eventually went their different ways . When that happened she thought she would never get over it , but of course she did .

After her stint at university, where she had achieved a business studies degree ,she got a job at an accountants office in the nearby town only a few miles from her home . She lived with her parents at the time . She had been in the accounts for a while and had started regularly socialising with some of the staff there . Once or twice a week they would all go to the local gym and it was there that she had met Ryan .He was a body builder and the resident fitness instructor. He was , tall , dark and handsome with a fantastic body and it wasn't until she thought she had fallen in love with him that she found out he was quite the ladies man . He had three girlfriends on the go at once and after a while she realised that he was actually rather vain . She felt really let down as it seemed that every time she was in a relationship that looked as if it was going to last , for one reason or another it fizzled out .

She was twenty-six years old now and was beginning to wonder if she would ever find

'the right one 'and get married and have a family . Maybe she would end up like one of her aunts , a lonely spinster , who had always put looking after her parents before her own happiness after she'd lost her fiance` in the second world war . Vicky didn't have a problem with her parents , they were very active even though they were nearing retirement age now , but although her two older brothers had produced grand-children for them , her Mum and Dad still nagged her about producing offspring of her own . Oh , well perhaps one day in the future , she pondered .

Her mind then flicked back to the present and she resumed looking for the little souvenirs

She thought a pack of Isle of Wight playing cards and a key ring would be ideal for her brother Jack , the one who was taking care of Snowy while she was away . For her brother David a commemorative coaster for the desk in his study . She bought some special packs of cookies for each of her sister-in-laws and then decided they would also be an ideal gift for her kind neighbours who were holding the keys and seeing to her rubbish bins while she was away. She pondered over some sticks of rock but thought better of it because her nieces and nephews teeth might suffer . Perhaps she'd buy them fudge instead . She picked up a bottle of chilled mineral water for herself and as she made her way to the till to pay for her purchases she reached over and took the special magnet from the stand that she had seen earlier . " Never know" she murmured to herself .

She was very pleased with all the things she had bought and took them back to the car . She knew they would be safer in the boot as the sun was getting hotter by the minute but she kept the small bottle of mineral water in her bag in case she needed it later .

She then went to look around some very interesting craft shops which were tucked away in a flag-stoned courtyard behind a very historic hotel and she marvelled at all the pretty thatched cottages in this part of town .

After enjoying the skill of the craft-makers she decided to cross the road and walked down to Shanklin Chine . It looked so cool and shady so she decided to go in . She paid the entrance fee and started down the gorge . The chine had been opened in 1817 , one hundred and ninety years ago , and it was the islands very first tourist attraction . It had a stream going right down to the beach with waterfalls coming down from the cliffs and Vicky felt a light breeze in the air as she walked down the steps. She went into the Heritage Centre and learned about PLUTO which was the <u>P</u>ipe <u>L</u>ine <u>U</u>nder <u>T</u>he <u>O</u>cean which had carried fuel to allied troops serving in Normandy during the second world war . There is also a memorial to 40 Royal Marine Commandos who trained in the chine for the Dieppe raids of 1942 . Vicky was overawed by all of this information and was so pleased she had decided to explore this attraction .

When she eventually reached the beach she went to find the lift ,she didn't think she could face walking all the way back up to the top , after all she was here for a rest .

By now Vicky was beginning to feel a little peckish and thinking back she remembered seeing a park with a café near the entrance to the chine , so she made her way back there thinking perhaps she could get some lunch .

As she climbed the steps into the park she could hear lots of birds chirping and suddenly in front of her she saw a large aviary filled with budgies , finches and cockatiels with the most amazingly colourful plumage . She loved birds and before she came away she had filled all the bird feeders to the brim in her little garden . Well she had enjoyed the aviary so she started towards the café . She ordered and paid for a ham salad and a coffee and because it was hot in the sun she decided to sit in a shaded area . The coffee cup was so cute , it had a matching spoon in the handle . She saw that they were for sale at the little shop there , in sets of four , so she made up her mind to buy a set and take them home to remind her of this lovely little place . She could see couples playing crazy golf in the café grounds and once again she felt quite lonely . She wondered once more if she'd be doing the same if she had a special man in her life .

She looked around the café grounds and saw that the owners had made the place look very welcoming by placing many brightly painted planters filled with very colourful flowering plants all around the little golf course . They were so beautiful and they enhanced the whole garden .

She was enjoying her lunch and while she sat there daydreaming she was suddenly aware of an old house through the trees . It looked empty and a little dilapidated and when she had finished here she decided to explore . Before she left the café she went to the counter and bought the set of mugs she had promised herself .

Vicky then strolled up the steps out of the café into the park beyond and was mesmerised to discover beautiful flower beds everywhere , which were all the colours of the rainbow . The park gardeners had obviously worked very hard to keep the displays in order . Vivid blooms in orange , yellow and red were basking in the early afternoon sunshine . What a difference the sunshine made . Vicky was so lucky she had chosen this particular time to come and the forecast was good for the whole fortnight .

She turned to the left and walked over to the old house . It looked a hundred years old and rather dilapidated . It had a wrought iron balcony completely surrounding the whole house upstairs and another downstairs . She could picture a Victorian family sitting out having afternoon tea and sunbathing . How magical this must have been when it was built . She walked towards the front door and climbed the front steps . She tried the door and was amazed to find it was unlocked and she knew she would not be able to resist peeping inside . The door opened into an elegantly designed hallway and there was a staircase with a wrought iron rail curling up in a spiral to the upper level . She gingerly crept up the stairs and peeped into each of the four bedrooms in turn and then she ventured into the bathroom . Although it was a little neglected it was still lovely . What memories these rooms must hold , she thought , feeling a mite guilty thinking about other peoples secrets . As she made her way back to the stairs she saw the door to the balcony but she thought it best not to chance going out because it looked rather unsafe . She proceeded back downstairs and there she found the remnants of a large family kitchen , a delightful dining room and a beautiful big lounge . There was another sitting room at the back with large French windows facing the sea . She peered out and was overawed by the view . The sky was cloudless and she glanced down at the still blue sea . The house was built on the top of the cliffs above Shanklin and Vicky thought that the panoramic view must have been the reason that prompted the original owner to choose this spot in the first place .

Suddenly she saw a movement in the garden and went back out of the front door closing it behind her . She walked around the side of the house towards the back garden . The garden was immaculate . How could an old empty house have such a beautifully well kept garden . As she walked towards the sea view a little voice piped up "And what do you think you are doing , young lady?" .

Vicky almost jumped out of her skin and whirled around to see the sweetest , yet most fragile looking old man she had ever seen ."Oh! I am so sorry" she was apologising as she walked towards him . He was very small and had grey hair and a pencil thin moustache . He was sitting in one of two deckchairs and was struggling to get up .

"Please don't get up" Vicky said .

"Well perhaps you'd like to come here and sit beside me , my dear " he nodded towards the empty deckchair.

Vicky walked over and sat herself down in the vacant seat beside him . She sensed he was a perfect gentleman and felt completely relaxed all of a sudden . She glanced at him and noticed that he had the most striking blue eyes that twinkled when he smiled .

"I'm Harry , by the way" his voice sounded like silk , as he held his hand out to take hers .

"Victoria" she said holding her hand out to shake his.

"I saw you in the house".

Vicky felt very guilty and apologised again but told him she couldn't resist it because the house looked as if it had such a mystical history and such magical memories.

"Oh it has" he pondered "and it's a very long story".

"Would you like to tell me about it?" asked Vicky "I would certainly like to hear it".

Harry's eyes were a little glassy with tears as he settled back into his deckchair and said "For me the magic started in 1941".

Harry had started to tell Vicky his life story .

Chapter 2.

VICKY listened intently as Harry told her he had been born in Westbury in Wiltshire in 1916 . His mother had previously been married to a miner and she and her husband had two little boys , Reuben and Johnny. Her husband had then been tragically killed in an accident at the mine in a small town nearby and she had been left a very young widow .

She had then met and married Harry's father in 1914 . But when Harry was just 18 months old his father was killed in France in the first world war and his poor mother was widowed again .

When Harry was old enough to go to work he went to the local glove factory and asked for a job . He was determined to work hard to support his mother who had always worked so hard herself to look after her three precious sons . He got the job and eventually completed a seven year apprenticeship to qualify as a cutter .

In 1939 when war was declared Harry was 23 years old and he asked his mother if he could become a sailor

. She was very distraught at the thought of him going to war but was also very proud that he wanted to fight for his country , so she agreed .

He applied to join the Navy but there were no positions available , so he joined the Army.

Then in 1941 when he discovered that the Navy needed some extra hands he was , at his own request , seconded to the Navy and at last he went to sea . His first long voyage , lasting about eight weeks ,was across the Atlantic to Canada and after a successful assignment they returned to Great Britain and on the way back Harry was overjoyed to experience the awesome Northern Lights .

After this epic voyage his ship had then patrolled the coast of Great Britain for quite a few months and at the end of August Harry's ship sailed into Liverpool . After months at sea the whole crew were happy to get some shore leave and it was great to be on dry land again .

On the Monday morning he decided to go to town . He was just passing a very high class baker's shop when he glanced in the window and saw a very pretty shop assistant behind the counter , so he thought he would go in .

He smiled at her and asked the price of the cakes . He later discovered that the assistant had felt sorry for him , a brave sailor fighting for his country and the likes of her , so she told him that the 2d cakes were 1d and the 5d cakes were 2d . He had decided on one of the more expensive ones and as he paid the 2d for it he had asked her name .

"Sarah" she'd replied and he had seen her blushing when he had smiled at her .

Harry had introduced himself and expressed how delighted he was to meet her as he held out his hand to shake hers.

She had wrapped his cake and handed it to him and she called out to him as he left the shop him saying that she hoped he would enjoy his purchase .

"Oh I certainly will" he had smiled and added "I hope to see you again".

Sarah told Harry many years later that she had then fetched a three-penny piece from her purse to put into the till to make up the difference in the price of the special cake that she'd sold to him , but she didn't mind , she knew it was worth it knowing how much he would enjoy the cake . Little price to pay , she thought , for Harry's dedication to his country .

Next day at the shop Sarah had been busily serving two elderly ladies with their strawberry cream treats for their tea when she looked up and saw four sailors coming into the shop . Harry had a few special friends on board and he had told them about meeting Sarah and about the superb cream cakes at the shop , so they thought they would pay a visit .

She recognised Harry and thought , oh crumbs , I hope they haven't come in for some more posh cakes . But they had , and after serving them and chatting brightly about all sorts of things from the war to the weather , they happily left with their box of fancy cakes.

Poor Sarah once again had to go to her coat pocket and take out a shilling from her purse and put it into the till to make up the difference for the cakes . Whatever was she going to tell her father if they came in again .At the end of the week her wages would be short and he would want to know why .

That evening as she was leaving the shop , Harry had emerged from the shadows and Sarah had nearly jumped out of her skin . He asked if he could escort her home and although she was a little reluctant at first she agreed he could walk her to the gate . When they arrived at the gate Harry asked if he might speak to her father . She was rather nervous but asked Harry to wait whilst she went inside.

When her father came out to see him Harry asked politely if he could take Sarah out the next day and was elated when her father agreed. The next day they had gone to the cinema and then had a cream tea for two at a really high class tea shop in the town .Years later in their life whilst reminiscing Sarah had told Harry that even then she had imagined them sitting in their own parlour with two chairs either side of the fire sipping tea together. On the way back to Sarah's house from the tea shop that day Harry had held her hand as they crossed a busy road and he never let go of it until they reached her house . That was when they had both realised that this relationship was definitely not a one off but was to be the start of a long and happy courtship.

Their first parting was quite traumatic for the pair of them and Harry had looked longingly and lovingly into Sarah's beautiful hazel eyes and murmured softly "I'm going to miss you so much , but I promise that when I get back I'll come to see you as soon as I can". Sarah hadn't realised that this was as hard for Harry as it was for her.

Sarah asked Harry if she could write to him

"I'd like that" Harry had replied with another of those devastating smiles . Then he asked her for a piece of paper and a pencil so that he could give her the details . He also gave her his home address in Westbury as he would be having some leave from Monday 8th September until Friday 12th and he wanted to see his family before he left on his ship to sail to the Mediterranean .

Harry then kissed her goodbye again and again and again and many times more before he had to tear himself away to get back to his ship on time . He waved goodbye as he went down the lane and Sarah had no idea how she held back the tears and had to go straight to her bedroom because she didn't want her mum and dad to see that she was so upset , although her mum would probably fully understand how she felt .

Years later she had told him that she had gone to bed feeling quite empty inside and already missing him terribly . She'd wished she had a best friend or a sister in whom she could confide because she was bursting to tell someone that she thought she was in love for the very first time in her life.

It was mid December before Harry got back to Liverpool and the weather was dreadful. It had obviously been snowing for quite a while but that didn't dampen his spirits . The ship had just docked at Liverpool and Harry was one of the first off . He hurried as fast as he could to the cake shop and found that Sarah wasn't there . The other assistant told him that it was her day off so he raced around to the house as fast as he could.

He had last seen her on the 2nd September and although they had exchanged many letters Harry had missed Sarah so much and it was still very hard to bear for both of them . Sarah had heard the knock as she was doing a little dusting . She could hardly believe it when she opened the door and saw Harry on the doorstep. Her face had lit up at the sight of him and her smile had shone like the sunshine . She asked him in but even before the door had closed Harry held had her in his arms and kissed her passionately . "I'm so sorry" he'd said as he ended the kiss , "but I've been waiting to do that ever since I last saw you".

Sarah told him she felt exactly the same.

After a few more months of long distant courting Harry promised that as soon as it was possible he would take her to meet his mother . His mother , Frances, had heard him talking so much about Sarah that she couldn't wait to meet her.

It was at Easter in 1942 that Harry eventually proposed to Sarah . He had taken her home to meet his mother on the Easter Saturday.

As Harry had introduced them Sarah had noticed a marked resemblance between the two of them. His mother was quite short , like Harry , but whereas he was slim his dear mother was as round as she was tall. She had looked really homely wearing her light green pinafore over a skirt and blouse. She had silver hair and glowing cheeks and she always seemed to be smiling .Harry had told Sarah that she had been through so much and had gone without so many things in her life to bring up her three sons , yet she always seemed eternally grateful for everything she did have. Sarah had thought at the time that considering everything she had endured she seemed a very happy soul indeed.

During the visit Harry had decided to take Sarah for a walk to Bratton , a village nearby and they headed up towards the Westbury hills .When they had reached the top they were completely exhausted and laid on the grass , side by side , looking up into the clear blue sky . The sun was shining and Sarah had stood up to look all around her , the view was amazing . "I feel as if I am on top of the world" she had sighed .

"You are my world" Harry had murmured softly .

Sarah had moved to come and sit down beside him , where he lay with his hands behind his head .

With a heart warming smile she had whispered tenderly "You say the nicest things , Harry", and she had stooped to kiss him gently on his lips . She then sat up and picked some daisies and made a chain which she placed around her neck .

Harry sat up and he picked a beautiful large daisy with a long stem and turned it onto itself and threaded it through to make a ring . He looked lovingly at Sarah and took her left hand in his .Then with the daisy ring hovering over the third finger he had proposed saying "I love you Sarah , more than anything else in the world ,and it would make my life complete if you would agree to become my wife".

There was only one obstacle to prevent them from marrying and that was her faith . Sarah was a Roman Catholic and she was unable to marry anyone of another faith. But she need not have worried because dear Harry already knew this and had converted to Catholicism without her knowledge

Sarah nearly cried , he sounded so sincere and always made her feel so special , as nobody ever had before so she had immediately accepted his proposal.

Her hands were shaking as Harry had placed the daisy ring on her finger , promising to make it a real one very soon . Sarah had wished that this little daisy ring would never die and that she could keep the special ring , as she would keep the memory of this special moment , in her heart forever .

Harry had then taken her gently into his arms and kissed her so tenderly that she couldn't stop the tears rolling down her face . He held her face in his hands then wiping away her tears with his thumbs , he looked straight into her sparkling eyes and pledged " I promise you here and now that we will always be together forever" he then kissed the remainder of her tears away and Sarah's heart seemed to sigh with contentment . She had never been so happy .

When they returned to the house his mother was overjoyed at the news , although with a war on it was anyone's guess how they'd manage to arrange a wedding , let alone afford it

Listening to Harry and Sarah's story was so poignant that Vicky found that the tears were rolling down her cheeks as Harry told Vicky that his mum had taken to Sarah instantly and after a while she had always looked on Sarah as the daughter she had never had .

"Oh , Harry this is such a beautiful love story".

"It's far from finished" said Harry continuing .

So it was that in the late spring of 1945 Harry had married his beloved Sarah in the lovely little church of St. Bernadette in Westbury in Wiltshire .

Sarah had worn a flowing white dress that she had bought second-hand , as many things like that were hard to come by near the end of the war. She had worn a floral head-dress that had a veil attached and had carried a delightful bouquet of carnations . Harry told Vicky that he couldn't resist glancing around at her as she had walked up the aisle with her father . She had looked amazingly beautiful .

Harry's eldest brother Reuben had been his best man and his niece's had been the little bridesmaids .

Sarah's parents and her brother Danny had travelled down , by train , the day before and Harry had arranged for them to stay for the week-end at his Aunt's house as her sons were still away in Burma and she had some spare rooms .

The reception was held at the church hall and although rationing meant that several things were scarce or even unobtainable they still had a marvellous time . The large one-tier wedding cake was beautiful and had been brought down by her parents It was a present from the owner of the cake shop where Sarah had worked in Liverpool .

They all had a fantastic day and when the party was over Harry took his lovely new wife to the Isle of Wight for a week for their honeymoon .

It was then during a walk along the cliff path above Shanklin that they had spotted the house . It was called 'Green Lawns' and Sarah had fallen in love with it from the first moment she'd set eyes on it . She told Harry that it would be her dream to live there with him forever .

Soon after they were married Sarah was pregnant with their first child , a daughter who was born in 1946 . They named her Judith . She was a bonny baby with dark hair and blue eyes like her Dad's .

Then to their joy in 1948 came Diana . Sarah was so sorry she hadn't given Harry a son to carry on the family name but Harry wasn't bothered . He simply adored his two little girls and as long as they were both healthy and strong he was happy . Their life seemed complete .

Whenever they could afford it they revisited the island for their annual holiday and each time they went up the cliff path in Shanklin to visit the magical house , as they had come to call it .As the girls grew up they came to love it and looked forward to seeing it on their trips . They were always sad when their holiday came to an end and they had to leave it all behind when they returned home .

When they returned from one particular holiday in 1951 and Harry went back to work there were rumours of redundancy and closures which worried Harry and Sarah immensely. Then in 1952 the bad news came .

After the war had ended Harry had gone back to work at the glove factory and eventually attained the position of head cutter , but now the factory was to close and he was to be made redundant . He was paid a large lump sum which he immediately put in the bank . He and Sarah thought it might cheer them up to go to the island again , so they took their two little girls and set off for a week . They never forgot the magical house on the cliff and as usual went back to see it . They just couldn't believe their eyes when they saw that it was up for sale . Harry made some enquiries and discovered that there were quite a few jobs available on the island and that with his redundancy money he could afford to buy the magical house for Sarah and she would realise her dream . They were so deliriously happy and within three months they had moved in .

Harry had got a job as a gardener at a large manor house on the island and the girls settled nicely into their new school and Sarah did lots of voluntary work at the church . Harry and Sarah had lived happily in the house for over 50 years .

Diana had married a local solicitor James Moore and had a son Adam who was Harry and Sarah's only grandchild . Diana and James had eventually purchased the house next door to her parents because they too loved the panoramic view and the surrounding area . They also felt they could keep an eye on Harry and Sarah if they lived nearby.

Judith had gone to live in America and had met and married a Texas oil millionaire but they had no children .

After many wonderful years together in their magical house Sarah had passed away after having a stroke . It had left Harry broken hearted and that was the reason he spent every afternoon in the garden . He sat in one of the deckchairs talking to Sarah whom he always imagined was sat beside him in the other chair .He then explained to Vicky that he was now living with Diana and James but couldn't part with the house because it held so many memories .

Chapter 3.

As Harry sighed after finishing his life story , which Vicky had been thrilled to hear , he suddenly looked behind her and saw his grandson walking across the lawn and called out "Adam come and meet my new friend , Victoria" .

" Please call me Vicky" she said as she started to turn around to face Harry's grandson

"Don't worry Grandfather , Vicky and I have already met".

To her absolute horror she turned around and saw the man from the supermarket restaurant . She immediately rose from the chair and began to apologise for her actions the previous day , but he just flashed that devastating smile of his and told her to forget about it and not to worry .

As he had strolled across the lawn to fetch his grandfather Adam had wondered who was sat in the deckchair beside him . As he drew near he had suddenly recognised that familiar mop of rebellious hair and his heart was performing double somersaults as the recognition hit him . Secretly he was so delighted to see her again . As he bent to help his dear grandfather out of the deckchair he chuckled to himself as the incident the day before had been the funniest thing that had ever happened to him .

Adam's mind then wandered back to the day before when he had first met Vicky . He had sat down at the last vacant table and then saw this vision of loveliness walking towards him . He couldn't believe his luck when she'd asked to sit with him . He had immediately noticed that she had beautiful grey eyes and that hair , oh how he would have loved to run his fingers through those amazingly unruly curls .

She hadn't realised herself but standing up on deck on the boat in the wind had made her hair look like a mop of candyfloss .

She had a superb figure and was wearing a figure-hugging top tucked into her jeans so he couldn't help noticing her pert breasts and trim waistline . Oh , Lord , he had suddenly felt quite aroused just looking at her , which surprised him because he hadn't felt like that for quite a while . She had such a charming smile and when she had settled herself down and picked up his chocolate bar he had almost burst out laughing . After they had finished the chocolate bar between them her face was so stern that he hadn't liked to say anything and then when she had taken that big bite out of his doughnut it had left a splog of cream on her nose . She had looked so cute he had wanted to kiss her . He would have loved to have seen her face when she discovered that the chocolate bar was his . He smiled again to himself .

"Come along Grandfather it's time for your tea".

"I must be going" said Vicky , trying so hard to think of any excuse to remove herself from this embarrassing situation .

"Oh , but Vicky must stay and have tea with us , son" piped up Harry.

"No , really I couldn't impose on you any more" she said meekly .

"I insist" said Harry "I've so enjoyed our chat and you wouldn't deprive an old man of a little extra company would you . It's okay talking to Adam here but he's not as pretty as you" he smiled with that twinkle in his eye .

"How can I refuse when you put it like that" she replied "the only problem is that I think my car park ticket must have expired by now" she looked at her watch with concern , "I'll have to go back and check".

"Then Adam will have to go with you and show you the road back up to the house , you can have free parking then so you can stay as long as you like". Harry grinned.

She smiled as they reached Diana's garden and Adam took Harry to a seat on the patio .

"We won't be long , Grandfather , I'll fetch your tea out for you now if you like".

"No I'll wait for you both" said Harry as he sat comfortably back in his chair looking very smug . He'd got his own way again and he had a feeling that things were going to work out just fine .

As they walked across the park Vicky once again told Adam how awful she had felt when she'd found her chocolate bar in her bag on the way back to the car .

"And what about my doughnut!" he laughed "I think I'm going to call you Doughnut from now on".

"You'll never let me forget it will you?" she said as she felt herself blushing again .

They had reached the road by now and Adam gently placed his hand in the small of her back as they crossed and suddenly Vicky felt a sensation of warmth pass right through her. Then her thought's went back to Sarah and the first time she had crossed the road with Harry . Had Sarah felt then as she did now .

Would she be seeing Adam again after today , she wondered .

They arrived at the car park with a few minutes to spare . Vicky unlocked the car and Adam sat in the passenger seat , then Vicky drove whilst Adam navigated until they arrived at the back of his parent's house .

Adam had explained in the car that he normally lived on the mainland , although he did own an apartment in Cowes for convenience when he came over to visit his parents or go sailing . He was staying at his parents home looking after Harry for a month whilst they had gone on a cruise . He was his own boss , he ran a very successful advertising agency with an office in Southampton , but as he could also work from home as well he had no trouble getting time off to look after Harry occasionally .

"You're rather young to be running your own company aren't you?" she enquired , fishing to find out how old Adam was .

"I'll tell you how old I am if you tell me how old you are first" he'd said with the wickedest of smiles .

"Oh , alright then", he'd made her laugh too . "I'm twenty six and a big bit".

"I'm suppose to say you don't look it now , am I?". She had blushed when he'd said that but as he'd looked at her , her fresh and flawless complexion had made him think exactly that.

"No , it was your turn to confess your age if you remember".

"Okay , you win , Doughnut , I'm thirty one and a little bit".

They collapsed into hoots of laughter thinking of the day before in the supermarket . Doughnut , what a nickname she thought , and as Vicky looked into his warm smiling eyes she felt a surge of emotion she had never felt before . She was so glad she'd met him again and so enjoyed just being with him .

They got out of the car and Adam led Vicky through the garden to where Harry was waiting for them , fast asleep . It was such a soft warm sunny day and he had used up loads of energy telling Vicky his life story so it was no wonder that he had dozed off .

Adam went to the kitchen to put the kettle on and he returned with the sandwiches he had made earlier and some super cakes ."I bought these at the supermarket yesterday" he joked . They talked quietly but Harry must have sensed that they were there and he woke up . "You weren't gone long" he yawned "let's have our tea and another long talk later".

After tea they moved through to the lounge and found so much to talk about . Vicky told them all about her fancy dress business and all the funny little stories that happen in a business like that . She also told them about Snowy her little pet . "Gosh , time flies when you're having fun" she said as she looked at her watch and saw that it was 8-30 pm "I must be getting back to Sandown" , yet all along she knew she didn't really want to leave.

"Have you decided where you'll be going tomorrow?" asked Adam .

"Not yet" answered Vicky deep down hoping he might suggest something . The thought of not seeing him again was unthinkable .

"Well perhaps we could take Grandfather to his favourite beach at Ryde . He hasn't been there for quite a while . Are you up for that Grandfather?" he asked with a smile .

"Too right" answered Harry "I haven't spent a day on the beach with a beautiful girl for years" Harry's face was a picture .

Nor me , Adam thought to himself , secretly thrilled at the thought of spending another day with Vicky .

"That's so kind of you both to ask me and I'd love to come . Shall I meet you there?"

"No" said Adam "we have to go through Sandown to get there so we'll pick you up . Is between 10-30 am and 11 am okay with you?"

"Sure , I'll look forward to that . Well I must be off then". She walked over to Harry's chair and stooped quickly down to kiss him on the cheek . She knew he would want to stand up but she also knew it was very difficult for him . "See you tomorrow then".

Harry beamed up at her "I can't wait".

Adam walked her out to the car and she was just about to get into it when he said "Don't I get a kiss on the cheek then , Doughnut?".

"I'll see you tomorrow" she said laughing "about 10-30 'ish . She got into the car and drove off , returning Adam's wave as she went . "Oh , he is so adorable" she said aloud as he went out of sight .

As she drove back to her apartment she thought back over the day and everything that had happened and knew she wouldn't have missed it for the world . She was so ecstatic to be seeing Adam again tomorrow and Harry , of course . She saw a lot of Harry in Adam , the kindness , thoughtfulness and the gentlemanly manners .She wondered as she parked her car , about Sarah and Harry's relationship and hoped that one day she would have a wonderful life like that herself .

Well she'd had plenty to eat today so she didn't have to cook anything so she decided to go for a walk before she retired for the night . She walked all along the promenade and stopped at the railings . She then took a long look at the sea , knowing exactly where her thoughts would be tonight , with a handsome young advertising executive called Adam Moore .

Next morning she was up early and after she had showered and dressed in a white floral dress and matching sandals she fetched a lightweight cardigan from the wardrobe in case the weather turned a little cooler later . She applied a little make-up , made her bed and then popped into the kitchen to make herself a light breakfast of fruit juice , toast and coffee . She suddenly felt so elated at the thought of seeing Adam again and she couldn't wait for the events of the day ahead to unfold .

She realised that she had actually been singing as she had made her bed . Then she thought about food for later and realised that they hadn't discussed that . She remembered that she and Adam had exchanged business cards last night so she rummaged through her handbag to find his number . She rang his mobile and was totally taken aback at her own reaction when she heard his husky voice on the other end of the phone .

"Hi , Adam Moore" he purred….silence…."Hello" he repeated .

"Oh , sorry Adam , it's me Vicky".

"Hi , Doughnut , is anything wrong?" he sounded quite perturbed .

"No" she was trying so hard not to let him sense the quivering in her voice "I just wondered if I needed to bring anything today?".

He felt very relieved as he replied "Well don't forget to bring your bikini and your suntan lotion , I think it's going to be quite hot today", he laughed as he thought , not just the weather either . He was visualising her in a two-piece swimsuit .

"I didn't mean that , I meant food or anything else we may need".

"Don't worry we'll eat out today . There's a lovely café and restaurant right beside the beach , at the spot we're going to . So we'll see you at about 10-30 then".

"Okay" said Vicky "I'm really looking forward to it".

And as Adam turned the phone off he said to himself "So am I , Doughnut , so am I".

Harry and Adam arrived at her little apartment on time and Vicky was on the front steps looking out for them . In no time at all she was getting into the car , "I'll sit in the back with Harry", she said hoping Adam wouldn't be offended but knowing that if she sat beside him it would be too close for comfort .

Harry smiled "I don't want to make Adam jealous". They all laughed and this light-hearted banter continued all the way to Appley Beach in Ryde .

When they had settled into their deckchairs on the sand Adam went to the little café to fetch some coffees .

"Sarah and I came here all the time when Judith and Diana were little" Harry mused "It was so safe for the children to paddle and play here in the shallow water . Then later when Adam arrived it was still our favourite beach . He loved it here too , watching the lifeboats and all the big ships coming and going , up and down the channel to Southampton or Portsmouth".

At that moment Adam arrived back with the drinks . "Talking about me Grandfather?".

"Just reminiscing about all our great days out here over the years , son".

Adam gave Harry a cup of coffee and placed the tray with the other two on the sand and laid down beside Vicky who was already stretched out sunbathing .

Then Adam sat up and offered to rub some sun bloc on Vicky's back "We don't want you getting burned". His hands felt so soft and warm as he touched her and she could feel an unbelievable sensation , almost like little electric currents , travelling all over her body as his hands moved sensually all over her back , down her arms and down the backs of her legs . Her imagination was running away with her at this moment as she silently wished , I don't want to be here with him , I want to be in a hotel room and feel more than his hands on me .

At the same time Adam was feeling unbelievably aroused as he caressed every part of her body that he possibly could without being indecent .

Suddenly she was brought back to the present when she heard Harry say "Are you asleep Vicky?".

"No I'm just resting my eyes" she sighed "and enjoying being mollycoddled".

"Well now it's my turn to be mollycoddled then" piped up Adam as he handed her the bottle of suntan lotion . She nearly died with ecstasy rubbing the cream all over his magnificent muscular back and his legs .

Suddenly he slowly turned over and looked into her eyes and he knew that massaging him was turning her to jelly . Adam almost hadn't turned over because he hadn't wanted his grandfather or Vicky to see that he was incredibly hard in his nether region . Her hands on his back and legs had felt so sensual and he had been imagining all sorts of sexual situations that he'd love to be in with Vicky at that moment and he'd wondered how long his resolve would hold out . "How about my chest , Doughnut , you missed that", he said flashing one of his knock-out smiles .

"Do it yourself" she said as she playfully threw the bottle of suntan lotion towards him. He then wrestled her down in the sand . How she wished they were lying alone together on the sand on a desert island , right now , what fun they could have . She could just picture them marooned and wondered what Adam might be doing to her right now in that situation . Her thoughts went back to the cruise ship and her day-dream , maybe Adam was the faceless stranger . Oh , how she wished…..

"Your coffee is getting cold , you two" Harry called to them , bringing them both back to reality. So they sat up and dutifully drank their coffee both knowing that the smouldering sexual tension between them was growing by the second .

After a while they began to feel hungry so they had a delicious lunch in the restaurant above the café . Then at around 3 o'clock they decided to pack up and go back .

Adam asked her if she would come back with them to his parents home as he would like to spend some more time with her but he didn't want to leave Harry on his own tonight . Somehow talking to Vicky about Sarah the day before and then the trip to their favourite beach had made Harry a little melancholy and Adam always worried about his beloved grandfather . She agreed , but Harry insisted that she sit in the front seat of the car with Adam on the return journey .

Vicky asked if it would be possible to pop back to her place in Sandown to fetch a change of clothes because hers were all covered in sand ."I think I could really do with having a shower".

"You can have one at our house" piped up Harry .

She didn't know if this was going to be a good idea .

Anyway they called at her apartment and she also decided to take all the perishables from the fridge . She had bought quite a few items and because she had spent such a lot of time with Harry and Adam she hadn't used much of it .

As she got back into the car with a couple of large carrier bags , one with food and the other with a change of clothes , she said "Tea is on me tonight , if that's alright with you both . I had such a lot in the fridge and I don't want to waste it".

They reached the house at about 4-00 pm and although Harry was exhausted he insisted that he would go into the garden next door for an hour or so . Vicky helped Adam prepare the evening meal and at 5-30 pm she went to call Harry . He was fast asleep and she didn't like to wake him , but just as she was walking away she heard him talking in his sleep to Sarah "Adam has found himself a nice young lady and I really think that they are going to be as happy as we were Sarah".

Vicky caught her breath , oh , I wish I could be as sure as you are , Harry , she thought , knowing then that she was falling hopelessly in love with Adam Moore . But how could she be , she had only met him two days ago .

Adam called out from next door , "Come on you two the dinner's getting cold".

Harry suddenly stirred "Oh , I must have dropped off for five minutes" he murmured .

"I just came to fetch you for your dinner Harry". She gently helped him to his feet and he held her arm as they slowly walked back to the house .

After dinner Harry decided on an early night .

"You don't mind if I take Vicky home and leave you here alone for a while do you , Grandfather?". Adam was always mindful of Harry .

"I don't know why Vicky doesn't stay overnight , there are enough bedrooms here" suggested Harry , "especially if you're thinking about going out together again tomorrow".

"That's a good idea actually ,Grandfather" he looked at Vicky "would you mind staying , it means I don't have to leave him for too long".

"I'd stay" she said "but I haven't brought any night clothes or a toothbrush with me". adding as an afterthought " Don't worry I can get a taxi back".

"But I'd like you to stay" Adam said softly "we could go for a walk along the cliff path and down onto the beach . Harry will be alright for half an hour and you could borrow some nightwear of mother's for later".

Protesting would seem futile at this point as both Harry and Adam seemed to have thought of everything.

"Alright I'll stay" she said , wondering if she'd made the right decision .

After Harry had settled down , Adam and Vicky left the house for their walk . It was getting a little darker now .

"Do you think it's wise going down the cliff path in this light?" she sounded nervous .

"It's well lit" answered Adam "and I've done it hundreds of times since I was a kid".

He helped her down and soon they were on the beach .Vicky took off her sandals and carried them . She loved the feel of the sand between her toes .

They found a large rock , sat and talked in general about different things and then Adam asked "Would you like to go out somewhere tomorrow?".

"I'd just as soon stay here" she replied " poor Harry will get too tired if we keep hauling him about everywhere".

He smiled "I think you've got a soft spot for my old grandfather".

"He is the nicest , kindest and most gentle man I have ever met" she said "I absolutely adore him and I wouldn't want him to get tired on my account".

Adam turned to look at her "I think you are the most delightful person I have ever met , Vicky" and he slowly lowered his mouth to hers and kissed her as gently as a feather floating down from the sky . Then as the kiss deepened she slowly melted inside until her heart felt like molten lava cooling down after a volcanic eruption . She uttered a long contented sigh as the kiss continued feeling as if they were joined like magnets never to be separated. The kiss became more powerful and intensified by the second. She didn't know how long the kiss lasted only that when it was over she knew she didn't want it to be . He held her so close that she just wanted to stay enclosed in his strong arms forever .

Suddenly a dog barked further along the beach and the kiss ended , bringing them both back to the present.

"We'd better be getting back in case Harry is worried about us", she knew that wasn't true but it was the first thing that came into her head .

So they trudged back over the beach towards the cliff path. Suddenly Vicky gave out a loud yell and she fell headlong onto the sand . She had stepped on a piece of jagged rock in her bare feet and also twisted her ankle as she fell.

Adam was quickly kneeling beside her "Oh , my poor darling" he said and proceeded to help Vicky to her feet.

Had she heard that right, even though she was in agony with her ankle , she loved the fact that he had just called her his darling .

"Can you put your foot to the ground" he had his arm around her waist holding her tightly.

"I don't think so" said Vicky grimacing .

So Adam picked her up in his strong arms and she felt elated as he carried her back to the house . He took her through to the lounge and placed her gently onto the sofa. "I'll just check on grandfather a second". Harry was asleep .

He came back into the room with a bowl of cold water and a facecloth . He soaked the flannel and wrapped it around her swollen foot . "It looks quite bad" he sounded very concerned "would you like me to take you to the hospital just to make sure you haven't broken it?" She nodded gratefully . Vicky didn't want to make a fuss but it was very painful . She was so glad that the jagged rock hadn't pierced her skin , it had only made her lose her balance .

Adam popped to the house next door and asked Bunty their neighbour if she could look in on Harry after an hour or so whilst he took Vicky to the hospital , St. Mary's , in Newport   Bunty didn't mind at all , she was a super neighbour .

As they drove to the hospital Adam felt very sorry for Vicky having her holiday spoiled with a sprained ankle but he was relishing the thought of playing nursemaid to her for the next few days .

At the hospital Vicky's leg was wrapped in quite a tight re-enforced elastic bandage and she was given crutches . "Do as you are told and you could get rid of these crutches in about three days and I need to see you again next week to take the dressing off." The Doctor spoke with authority "Do you have anyone to look after you?"

"I'll be taking care of her" Adam's deep voice came from behind her . His lips then came so close to her ear he could have kissed it , "If that's alright with you , of course?" he whispered . She couldn't see his smile but she felt it , and she didn't need to answer he could see by the look in her eyes that she wanted to be with him as much as he wanted to be there for her . Then she said "I don't want to be a bother".

He just looked at her and smiled again and said "As if ."

Chapter 4.

Harry was thrilled that Vicky was staying for a few days and as he watched the two of them together he could see a special bond developing . They played Scrabble and Monopoly all morning on the Tuesday , then both Harry and Vicky went into the garden of the magical house in the afternoon . Adam first carried Vicky across then came back to help Harry . Sitting there in the deckchairs with Harry , in the soft sunshine , was so very relaxing . I'm enjoying this , she thought .

They were talking about the view and saying how beautiful it was when they saw three ships sailing up the channel towards the Solent ."They look as if they are in a convoy" said Vicky .

"I have been in many a convoy" said Harry "I remember in 1941 I was in a convoy of about fifty ships and we were attacked by the enemy . It was on the 24th of May and one of our ships , The Hood , took a direct hit and sank . There were over 1400 men on that ship and only three survived" Harry's voice was tinged with sadness "I often think about the sailors who died and thought that there but for the grace of God go I . Anyway" Harry continued "the enemy ship that sank her was called The Bismarck . We shadowed her for three days and eventually got our revenge . She was finally sunk on 27th of May 1941 . How lucky I was Vicky to survive the war when so many didn't", he sighed .

"I'm so very pleased you did make it Harry or I wouldn't have met you and enjoyed sitting here listening to all your stories". or met Adam she smiled to herself .

"My own father died in World War I . I was only 18 months old when he died so I never knew him . Eventually Sarah and I were lucky enough to discover that his grave had been traced to Ypes in France . So in 1986 we travelled to Ypes to place flowers on his grave . Anyway we mustn't be morbid , let's talk about something else" he smiled , patting Vicky's hand as he said it .

Harry has such a captivating smile , thought Vicky .

"Why do you keep the house?" she enquired trying to change the subject to something less gloomy "is it because of all the memories , only it seems such a shame that this lovely house is lying empty".

"Do you like the house , Vicky?"

"Oh , I love it , but you didn't answer my question".

"I cannot bear to think of anyone else living here whilst I am still alive because I wouldn't be able to sit here with Sarah everyday and I think that would kill me".

"Oh , Harry" said Vicky softly , and she held his hand in hers for a moment .

"Diana's house is really lovely" Vicky added quickly when she saw tears forming in Harry's eyes .

"Yes , Diana and James bought it not long after they were married so that they could be near to us . I couldn't have managed without them , especially when Sarah was ill , and of course now I live with them . I'm so lucky to have such a wonderful family and to have my lovely sitting room overlooking the sea , just as I did in my old house" he said indicating behind him .

Vicky had been shown around Adam's parents house the first night she had stayed . From the front it looked like a big doll's house . It had a central front door with two large bay windows on either side of it on the ground floor . The bays then continued up to the next floor so that each of the two bedrooms facing the sea also had large bays . It meant the view was fantastic from each one of them .Both front bedrooms had en-suite bathrooms . The guest bedroom , in which Vicky was sleeping , and Adam's bedroom , both at the back of the house , had a bathroom situated between them which they were sharing at present . There was a stair lift installed to make it easier for Harry .

The night before when they had returned from the hospital and Adam was about to take her up to the guest room he had asked if she wanted to use the stair lift . She only had to look at him with those beautiful grey eyes of hers and he had scooped her up into his arms and carried her . She liked that much more and she was sure that Adam didn't mind either

Downstairs at the back of the house was a superb dining room . It had a large mahogany table in the centre with eight beautiful carvers . The pendant light came down low over the table and the subdued lighting was quite romantic . There were French windows leading from the dining room into a spacious conservatory . The kitchen was sublime , very large , with attractive units and all mod cons . It also had an island of units in the centre , every women's dream , thought Vicky when she'd first seem it .

Vicky's thoughts returned to the present and she realised that Harry had fallen asleep . She decided to close her eyes for just a moment and couldn't believe it when Adam came a while later to call them for dinner . They had both slept for over an hour .

Adam asked his grandfather to wait a minute whilst he carried Vicky back to the house in his arms . He sat her at the dining table and popped back to fetch Harry .

Whilst he was gone she thought how marvellous it was to hold on to Adam as he carried her back across the garden . Vicky wasn't the type of person to like being fussed over but she was loving ever minute of Adam's attention and she felt she wanted to be in his arms forever , but then she thought there wasn't much chance of that at the moment .

When Adam had helped Harry back to the house and sat him down beside Vicky they found that Adam had cooked them a scrumptious dinner . Gammon steak with pineapple, salad and jacket potatoes . Vicky had never felt so spoiled but decided to enjoy every minute of it . After devouring a large portion of lemon meringue pie and fresh cream for dessert she was almost too full to move . "That was absolutely delicious" she said as she heartily congratulated Adam on the superb meal "where did you learn to cook like that?".

"Comes with living on your own most of the time" he answered sullenly.

Vicky was thinking that perhaps his single status at the moment was not exactly as he would have wished it.

Vicky offered to help Adam with the dishes but he would have none of it , so she and Harry went through to the lounge to have another chat . Harry picked up the crutches and handed them to her . She was getting used to them now but although she was taking pain-killers she found her ankle was still very painful . They settled down on the comfortable sofa and she couldn't believe they could still find so much to chat about but Harry always came up trumps with another one of his stories .

After a couple of hours Harry decided to go to bed , so Vicky kissed him on his cheek and Adam helped him to the stair lift and then to his bedroom .When he returned he sat on the sofa beside her where they talked about things in general and then Adam told her he had a boat and belonged to the local yacht club in Cowes. "When you feel better and you have got rid of those crutches perhaps you'd like to come sailing with me next week?"

"That would be great" she sounded very enthusiastic "but I'm rather tired now so I think I'll turn in".

He immediately rose from the sofa and helped her to her feet . He then lifted her into his arms and took her to the guest bedroom . He gently lowered her onto the bed and asked if there was anything that she needed . She couldn't tell him what she was actually thinking at that precise moment , that she wanted him to join her in the bed and make slow yet mad passionate love to her . She was imagining his strong manly hands meandering their way down her naked torso when she heard him say "I'll just pop back downstairs and fetch your crutches in case you need to use the bathroom".

After returning with the crutches he gave her a little peck on the cheek and said goodnight

As he closed the door she let out a great sigh of frustration then reached for the crutches and went to use the bathroom .

As she lay in bed that night she couldn't sleep at first , thinking about everything that had happened since Sunday . Why had he kissed her so passionately on the beach and yet now he kissed her as if he was her brother . She was sure he liked her . Oh , why did she love him so . As she thought about this she slowly drifted into sleep .

By Thursday Vicky was able to manage without the crutches , so Adam decided it would be a good idea to take them both , Vicky and Harry , to Ventnor to the botanical gardens there . It was set in 22 acres of grounds with beautiful lawns and flower beds . The whole place was bursting with colour and because of the mild climate it housed many sub-tropical and exotic plants , shrubs and trees . Adam told her that many of the species grown here could not be found anywhere else in the country .Vicky loved plants so she knew she would enjoy this trip immensely . Also Harry had told her how he used to grow all his own plants when he'd worked at the Manor house as gardener , so he was a wealth of information as well .

They couldn't walk very far but there were plenty of seats where the two of them could sit down . Vicky felt very sorry for Adam being stuck with two invalids this week , but he didn't seem to mind and he had said that the fresh air would do them all a power of good .

Little did Vicky know but he was only too pleased to be spending time with what was fast becoming the two most important people in his life .

They took great pleasure in the spectacular views of the coast and managed to make it to the café where they thoroughly enjoyed a delicious lunch . Then Vicky spent some time perusing the contents of the little gift shop and purchased a few more souvenirs to take home . She had realised that she had forgotten to get something for her dad in the gift shop at Shanklin on Sunday but as she looked around there were several things that she knew he would like . She saw some rather nice mugs with a map of the island and as her dad loved a nice cup of tea in as large a cup as possible she thought that this would be perfect for him .

On the way back Vicky suggested a take-away for dinner to save poor Adam doing all the cooking again , as he still wouldn't let her help him . He agreed it was a good idea and said that he would order it later and have it delivered . Then he asked if she minded if they returned to the house now because Harry would want his little rest in the garden .

She didn't mind at all and thanked Adam so much for taking them out .The weather had been marvellous and she'd had such an enjoyable day .

On Friday Harry told them he would be fine if they would like a day out , just the two of them together . Both were reluctant to leave him on his own , but after a little persuasion they asked Bunty next door if she could look in on Harry at lunchtime and make him a cup of tea . She was only too pleased to help. Before they went out they made Harry some sandwiches and left them in the fridge .

That day Adam took her to Totland Bay . There was not a lot there but it was quiet and it was lovely just ambling along the seafront . They were the only ones there , not another soul in sight and Vicky was just thrilled to have Adam completely to herself.

As they walked a slight breeze blew up "You're not too cold are you?" as always Adam was very thoughtful .

"I'm okay , I just wish I had brought some gloves" she rubbed her hands together as she spoke .

"Come here , let me warm them for you" he opened his coat and motioned her to put her hands inside . She did so , wrapping her arms all around him . "That's better , now I have you just where I want you" he said smiling as he enfolded her in his arms and he lowered his lips to hers and gave her the tenderest of kisses . Vicky was in ecstasy and her legs almost gave way .

Adam finished the kiss quite suddenly "Come on , I know a place where we can get a piping hot drink and you can wrap your hands around the mug and get warm". He caught hold of her hand and ever mindful of her sore ankle he led her slowly back along the seafront to a small café , which she had seen on the way along .

But I was quite happy getting warm as I was , she thought and she could almost feel herself pouting .

Adam had been to the café before and he knew that they baked delicious jacket potatoes and as he was quite partial to the prawn variety he thought he would like one for lunch . He asked Vicky if she would like one as well and as she loved them , she said yes but decided that she would like coleslaw on hers with grated cheese on top and of course he ordered the mug of tea to wrap her hands around . Her thoughts kept going back to the kiss and she wondered if he was thinking the same .

They left the café and Adam took her hand in his as they walked back to the car ."Feel better now , Doughnut?"

"Very much better , thank you". Although deep down she still would have liked to continue where they left off with the kiss .

When they were settled in the car he asked "Would you like to visit a really good pottery , it's on the way back".

She smiled and said she'd love to , hoping that there wouldn't be too much walking . So he drove her to the Chessel Pottery near Calbourne .

Vicky had never seen such beautiful figures . Apparently the original owners had come from abroad and had brought the method of making it with them . She absolutely adored the Unicorn she saw . It looked like smooth white porcelain on the body of the horse and was decorated all around the head , neck and base with beautiful small pink flowers. It was so delicate . She had to buy it and anyway pink was her favourite colour . Then she saw the Pegasus , the winged horse ,in the same design and couldn't decide which one to have . They were very expensive and although she really could afford it she thought that buying both would be a little extravagant . Anyway she opted for the Unicorn because it seemed more enchanting and magical . She also bought her mother a pretty trinket box .

As they went back to the car Adam handed her the keys ."Let yourself in" he excused himself "I'm popping back to the loo".

He came back to the car five minutes later with a carrier bag in his hand and as he got into the driving seat he handed it to her "A little present for you" he said smiling .

"You shouldn't have!" she exclaimed and as she opened it she almost knew it was the Pegasus . She was thrilled but chided him for spending so much money on her . At least it gave her an excuse to give him another kiss to say thank you .

"It was my pleasure" he said . Was he talking about buying her the present or the kiss . Even now just sat beside him , he aroused feelings in her that she had never felt before and she just wished so hard that he would take it further .

On Saturday Adam said that he had to go to the supermarket to stock up the fridge and the larder . They looked at one another and giggled , thinking about what had happened in the supermarket restaurant just one week before .

So much had happened to Vicky herself that week but she was so glad it had . Except of course for the ankle injury , that was still so painful , but if it hadn't happened she perhaps wouldn't have spent so much time here with one very interesting man and one very sexy one .

She didn't go with Adam as he thought she may find it too much , walking up and down the aisles . When he mentioned that word she thought there was only one aisle she would like to walk down with him but of course she didn't say anything .

She sat in the garden again with Harry . He still told her funny little stories that had happened to him and Sarah over the years . He told her that one winters day he had gone into his garden and saw something in his greenhouse . He had wandered over and opened the door and saw a tramp asleep on the floor . The squeak of the door had woken the tramp and Harry asked "What are you doing here , my son" . the tramp had got up and apologised to Harry and told him that it was so cold the night before even the greenhouse was warmer than sleeping outdoors under the stars . Harry felt so sorry for him and he invited him into the kitchen where he and Sarah had made the tramp tea and toast . The tramp was so very grateful .

Vicky had just heard another example of Harry's kindness and thought it a great shame that there weren't lots more men in the world like him .

Adam soon returned and they put all the shopping away . They must have looked like a married couple living in the same house doing the chores together . The thought crossed her mind and she liked it very much .

They spent the next couple of days sightseeing and enjoying each others company immensely . Sometimes Harry went with them and other times he sat in his garden and Bunty made his tea . Harry was quite happy to let them go off on their own , very happy indeed , he thought with a twinkle in his eye .

Vicky decided on the Tuesday morning to go back to her apartment in Sandown . Adam had taken her back to the hospital to have the elastic bandage removed and to return the crutches .

As he pulled up outside the house , she saw her little red car looking lonely and forlorn . She asked him if he would like to come inside for a drink . He said he would love to so he came in and stayed for a couple of hours . The whole time he was there Vicky didn't know how she would cope . She was in the kitchen making some cold drinks because she had forgotten that she had no milk and her mind was going into overdrive. He was so gorgeous , she thought , and she so wanted to make love with him . Was he waiting for her to make the first move . No , she would be so embarrassed if he turned her down . Perhaps he didn't make love in the middle of the day , maybe he was strictly a night-time guy . Her mind was in a complete whirl thinking up all the excuses under the sun why he would or would not want to make love to her .

She came through to the lounge from the kitchen and they sat talking about mundane things and he said he liked the apartment . He also told her that his parents were due back from their cruise the next day which was Wednesday .

As they were washing up the tumblers he asked her if she would like to go sailing on the Thursday as he would have finished his grandfather-sitting by then . She told him she'd like that very much .

Adam said he'd better be getting back to Harry so she saw him to the door and he kissed her lightly on the cheek . After he had gone Vicky sat in silence in the little sitting room with her eyes closed re-living everything that had happened over the last eleven days . She could hardly believe the coincidences and thought that fate must have played a big part in all of this , but was it going to be completely platonic between her and Adam or was something earth shattering about to happen...she wished .

Although she'd had a wonderful time staying with Adam and Harry she thought back over her time there and realised that Adam had just kissed her goodnight gently each evening when she went to bed , just like she had kissed Harry . The kiss on the beach had been the deepest and longest he had given her , then there was the sweet kiss at Totland Bay . How did he really feel about her , she thought . She knew she loved him more than life itself and even thinking about him now aroused sensational feelings throughout her whole body . She had never felt this way about any man before . Time was moving too fast and all too soon she would be going home . She was suddenly racked with panic and her heart was pounding . She didn't want to go back , she didn't want this wonderful thing with Adam to end . Oh now she was being silly , pull yourself together Vicky , she told herself and she came back to reality with tears rolling down her cheeks . She got up from the sofa and cheered up a little when she remembered that Adam said he would pop back that afternoon and take her out again .

Meanwhile as Adam was driving back to Shanklin he couldn't get Vicky out of his mind . He had so wanted to sweep her up into his arms , take her to bed and make love to her today at her apartment but he wasn't sure how she felt about him and he couldn't bring himself to take advantage of her . She had responded to his kisses but perhaps she had just been taken up by the heat of the moment when that had happened . He still had two days left with her …maybe…he could only hope .

Adam arrived back to pick her up , as arranged at 2 pm . He had told Vicky to wear casual clothes so she wondered what he had in store for her . He drove them to Alum Bay on the south west coast of the island . Where ever you were on this lovely island it didn't take long to travel anywhere else .

She had never been to a place like this before and was most fascinated to witness the glass blowing at one of the many craft workshops. What a skill these men had making beautiful decorative glassware from lots of hot blobs . After looking around some of the other small workshops Adam asked if she would like to ride on the chair lift . She said okay so he bought the tickets and they walked towards the chairs . They sat close together and were strapped in . Suddenly the chair was going over the edge of the cliff and Vicky felt herself fill with panic and her stomach seemed to be in her mouth . She screamed and Adam laughed , then he put his arms around her and she buried her head in his chest and didn't surface until the chair stopped at the beach . Although she was scared to death it didn't stop her from breathing in the scent of him and loving it . He asked if she was alright and gave her a little kiss on her cheek and hugged her tightly .

Oh how safe she had felt in his arms .

"Shame you missed the view" he grinned .

"I'm so sorry" she said feeling embarrassed "but I've never been on a chair lift before and I didn't think I would be this frightened". She felt her heart beating furiously or was it the effect of being so close to Adam that had caused it .

"Well it's just as well your knight in shining armour was here to save you" he said with a wide smile .

"Thank you kind Sir" she said laughing and suddenly she felt a little more relaxed .

They walked along the beach and Adam suggested a boat ride around the Needles which she thoroughly enjoyed .

They rode on the chairlift again but this time she was more prepared and it didn't feel so bad going up , but Adam cuddled her again "just to be on the safe side" he assured her smiling . Little did he know how much she loved it .

On their way back to the car park they passed a shop which sold coloured sand . Together they filled two little containers , which were shaped like a map of the island , with different coloured sand and then put the liquid in and sealed them . Adam went to pay but Vicky stopped him "No" she insisted "I'll pay for one and you pay for the other and then we'll swap them and it will be a present to each other to remind us of this trip".

He agreed smiling but thought , how will I ever forget being anywhere with you , my darling Doughnut .

On the way back in the car Adam asked if she would come back with him to have dinner with Harry and himself that evening .

"Of course , thank you" she replied , unable to resist spending time with this guy who was gradually growing on her more each day . "You won't mind if I don't stay over again , you said your parents will be back tomorrow and I don't want to intrude".

"You would never be intruding , Doughnut , you know we'd love you to stay".

"That's very kind of you but I would prefer to come back to the apartment tonight . If you like you can drop me off at the house in Sandown and I can drive up later" but before she could say anything else Adam interrupted.

"It's no trouble to take you back after dinner , I'm still worried about that ankle of yours . I know you will have to drive you car soon but perhaps another couple of days resting it will help". He was just trying to think of any excuse to see more of Vicky before she went home on Saturday . "Anyway don't forget we're going sailing on Thursday".

"I haven't forgotten , in fact I'm really looking forward to it . Also thanks so much for today , I'm thrilled with my little present" she was referring to the little sand island that they had made .

"Me too" he replied .

They chatted in general about the afternoon and before she knew it they were back at his parent's house .

"I'll go and put the kettle on . Would you mind going to see if Grandfather is in the garden next door , I expect he asked Bunty to take him across earlier".

Vicky walked across the lawn and realised why the magical house was called 'Green Lawns' , they looked so lush and green .

She suddenly saw that both deckchairs were empty and hurried back to the house . Adam was in the kitchen.

"Do you think Harry is alright , only he's not in the garden" she said as she came through the back door sounding a little panicky.

Adam suggested that she look in his sitting room but he wasn't there either . Adam searched upstairs , no Harry. So they both hurried to Bunty's .

There was Harry laughing and chatting to Bunty's Uncle Henry . Henry had been a sailor in World War 2 and although they had never met before they had a lot in common . Bunty apologised for not leaving a note to say she had brought Harry home with her . "You're back earlier than I thought , I hope you've both had a lovely time."

Vicky and Adam both nodded .

Harry was so engrossed in his conversation with Henry that he hadn't even noticed their presence .

"Leave him here until his dinner's ready if you like" suggested Bunty "Henry has to start back soon and it seems a shame to interrupt their reminiscences".

"Thanks , one of us will pop back in about an hour then". They said goodbye and walked back through the adjoining gate to the garden . Quite naturally it seemed Adam reached for her hand and held it tightly as they returned to the back door . "I hope that Spaghetti Bolognese is alright for tonight , it's quick and easy to prepare".

"Please let me help you , I feel so useless" she pleaded.

"But you're on holiday , you should be pampered . Saturday will be here soon enough and you'll have to go back to work , so take advantage of me and my culinary skills while you can" he laughed as he reached into the fridge and cupboards to get the ingredients .

I wish I could take advantage of you , she thought , but not in the kitchen . Then the thought of going back on Saturday hit home and she sensed a sick feeling low in her stomach . She didn't want to leave and she felt herself becoming visibly distressed so she mentally told herself to calm down or Adam would notice and she couldn't possibly tell him what was wrong .

When the dinner was ready they collected Harry and all through the meal he told them about his afternoon talking to Henry . He was so elated but also very tired .

Immediately after the meal they cleared the table and loaded the dishwasher . Then Vicky told Harry she was going back to Sandown that night but she would be back to see him before she went home on Saturday to say goodbye .

Adam asked if he would be alright whilst he took Vicky back and Harry nodded . He seemed quite sad that she wasn't staying for the rest of the week .

They were both a little quiet going back in the car , although Adam did ask her what she would be doing the next day .

She said she would probably have a look around Sandown and visit the pier and make sure she had all the little gifts she was taking back with her . She had yet to buy something for her friends Liz and Brian .

When they arrived at the apartment he said he wouldn't stay because he was worried about leaving Harry for too long . She understood . He got out of the car and went around to the other side and opened the door for her and as she straightened up he kissed her lightly on the lips and told her he would ring her the next day to arrange what time to pick her up on Thursday to go sailing . He watched her go up the steps to the front door and as she let herself in he waved then got into the car and drove away .

Vicky went up to the apartment and felt very lonely on her own . She had come on holiday to get away from it all but she hadn't banked on meeting Harry and Adam and seemingly getting so involved with them . She had booked this place for a fortnight and had only spent a couple of days here .

Her thoughts continued to linger on those two special men and on how much she had enjoyed spending time with them both . She went into the kitchen to make herself a drink and then realised she had no milk . She had taken all her perishables to Adam's last week and had completely forgotten to get some more on the way back today . She put her coat back on and went out hoping she may find a shop open to buy some .She walked along the promenade and felt almost like she did on her first night here . She couldn't get any milk so she went into a café that was still open and ordered herself a latte . She sat near the window and looked out at the sea , oh how she loved it here! She finished her drink and paid at the till then walked back to her apartment. She went to bed that night knowing that she would dream about Adam , well that was if she got any sleep at all .

Chapter 5.

NEXT morning she slept in until after 9-30 am . She got up , showered and dressed in slacks and a fluffy jumper . Although it was May some days could feel a little chilly in the morning and then it warmed up later on . She had no milk for cereal or coffee and no bread so she put on her coat and walked along the promenade to the café she had found the night before .There she enjoyed a fruit juice , a full English breakfast with eggs , bacon , sausages , tomatoes , hash browns and fried bread . Goodness she hadn't had fried bread for years and it was just how she liked it crispy and scrunchy . That was followed by toast and marmalade and a lovely piping hot cup of tea .she really enjoyed it and felt full to the brim . I had better walk this off she thought after paying the bill .

She left the café behind her and made her way towards the pier . When she reached it she saw that there was a variety show on that night and she thought she might enjoy that , so she went to the booking office and purchased a ticket .

Her day passed very quickly and at about 6 pm her mobile phone rang . She guessed it was Adam because after her initial call home to let her Mum know that she had arrived safely , she had asked her Mum to tell everyone that she didn't really want to be disturbed for the rest of her holiday and her family and friends respected that . It was Adam . He asked how she was and had she had an interesting day . She told him what she had done and also said she was getting ready to go to the show on the pier . She thought he may have suggested joining her but he didn't , perhaps he had seen enough of her in the last two weeks and needed some space . But then he said he had rung to arrange to pick her up next morning for the sailing trip and she felt awful thinking such a thing .

"Will 10 o'clock be alright with you?"

"Fine" and after asking after his parents and Harry she rung off .

The show was great and really cheered her up . There was a comedian who was very funny although she had heard some of the jokes before . Also a competent pianist , a very talented singer and wonderful dancers , and with the audience participation it was an all round super show . She was so glad she decided to go , it had cheered her up immensely.

Vicky ambled slowly back to the apartment and before she went to bed she set the alarm for 8 am . She didn't want to keep Adam waiting in the morning .

Adam arrived at 10 am , he rang the door bell which made Vicky jump , she hadn't heard it before . She was all ready and made her way down to the front door . She was wearing jeans and a tee-shirt and she had on a short quilted jacket and she also wore flat shoes . As she opened the door he flashed that gorgeous smile of his and kissed her on the cheek .

"Am I alright in this ?" she pointed to her outfit .

"You'll do" he answered smiling "if you need anything else I've probably got it on the boat . You've remembered your bikini , I hope".

She nodded but felt herself blush a little .

She made sure the front door was locked then he walked her to the car and opened the door for her . As he was walking around to his side of the car she thought how handsome he looked . He had on jeans , a dark crew necked sweater and deck shoes . He looked every bit the sailor .

He got in and they drove to Cowes . He parked the car and asked her to wait whilst he reported to the Harbourmaster's office . She presumed he had to tell them where he was going . When he returned she got out of the car . He went to the boot and removed several bags "Provisions for later" he said . He seemed to think of everything , she thought .

They walked along the dock passed some enormous boats and Vicky felt her mouth drop open when Adam stopped and turned to help her aboard this fabulous yacht .

"Is this yours!" she asked absolutely astounded by what she saw .

He then explained that his grandfather on his father's side had been an avid sailor . Adam had spent many years , from when he was just a lad until he was grown up , sailing with his grandfather and as Adam was the only one interested in the boat , it had been left to him when his

Grandfather Moore had died . His paternal grandfather had adored his wife so much that when he had the yacht built it was named after her . The boat was called the

Lady Eleanor . It was white with a large sail which Adam had to hoist later .

He took her below and she saw that there were two cabins as bedrooms with proper beds , not bunks , a beautiful lounge and a super kitchen which he said was called the galley . She knew really but she thought she would humour him a little .

They eventually got underway and after about an hours sailing he steered into a small bay which seemed very secluded . He dropped the anchor and then they both settled down on the deck to drink the delicious cocktails which he had prepared in the galley below . By now she had changed into her bikini because the sun was becoming very hot in this sheltered bay . They decided to go swimming .

"I'm not a very strong swimmer" she confessed .

"Don't worry" he re-assured her "I'll stay close to you". he was already feeling quite hot and bothered just looking at her in that revealing red bikini , and being this close to her worried him a little because he didn't know if he could trust himself to keep his hands off her . They swam and played in the water and several times he took her in his arms and kissed her lightly on the lips . Oh , how she wished at this moment that he was not such a gentleman , that he would take her and ravish her . She imagined him as an old-fashioned Errol Flynn type pirate carrying her onto the deck and making wild erotic love to her .

"Vicky….Vicky".

"Oh , sorry I was far away then" she said as he let her go .

"It's almost lunch-time , are you hungry?".

Only for you she thought .

They climbed aboard , helped each other dry , then settled into the chairs to eat the mouth-watering salmon sandwiches and fruit that Adam had so thoughtfully brought with him . He opened a bottle of sparkling white wine . Vicky didn't drink much alcohol but if she did have a drink it was always sparkling white wine . How would he know she liked that , she pondered , or maybe he gave this to all of his women .

After lunch they just lay on the padded double sun-bed and she felt so aroused she decided to take the bull by the horns and go for it . She turned over and looked at Adam . Was he asleep , she wasn't sure but she moved towards him anyway and gently kissed him full on the mouth . He certainly wasn't asleep as he returned the kiss with passion . It grew much deeper and more urgent and suddenly Vicky felt as if a fire was erupting inside of her and then......a mobile phone was ringing.... So he ended the kiss and sat up "So sorry , Doughnut", I told my secretary that if anything urgent cropped up she could ring me".

He went further up the deck to answer the phone and talked business for about ten minutes , which to Vicky seemed like an hour . The magic of the kiss had evaporated and the moment was lost forever . She sat there wondering what would have happened if the phone hadn't rung .

When he returned she suggested they go for another swim as she needed to cool off . She immediately stood up and dived straight in which she had never done before but Adam followed her and they surfaced together .

He was also glad to cool off . When Vicky had turned over to kiss him he had been taken a little by surprise . He was not the kind of man who pushed himself on a woman but he was so glad she had made that move , it opened up a way to begin the subtle seduction that he had been longing for ever since he had met her .

Later that afternoon he told her he had brought a barbecue along and did she want to go ashore and together they could cook their evening meal on the beach . She agreed it was a good idea but she didn't want everything to get wet wading ashore . She had not realised that attached to the back of the boat was a dingy which would take them ashore .

They had a lovely evening and she felt like Robinson Crusoe on a desert island as they were quite alone on the beach . The beach had huge cliffs around it and it was only accessible from the sea . Maybe this was a fitting substitute for the island that she had day-dreamed about before .

It was beginning to get dark so they packed everything up and took the dingy back to the boat . Vicky was expecting them to return to Cowes but Adam asked her to stay the night on the boat ."But I haven't brought any nightwear with me".

He eyed her very seductively and asked "Do you need any?"

She smiled at him as she shook her head "I suppose not".

He then took her into his arms and kissed her profoundly . She opened up to him and the kiss deepened further . He began to undress her and she him and when they were both naked on the deck he swept her into his arms to carry her below . As he reached the cabin door he looked very lovingly into her eyes and asked "Are you sure this is what you want?"

She didn't answer but just kissed him passionately as he pushed open the cabin door , entered then kicked it shut behind him . He lay her on the bed and just gazed at her for a moment before telling her how beautiful she was . Then he lay beside her and their lovemaking began in earnest .

Vicky woke from the most wonderful dream and wondered where she was for a moment . Then she realised it was not a dream and she let out a huge sigh . Last night had been the most sensational night of her entire life . Adam had taken her to bed and had sensually kissed her from her neck to her knees and with his words and actions had made her feel as if she was the most beautiful woman in the whole wide world .

How was she going to walk away from this . It was only a holiday romance and Adam didn't seem the type to settle down . After this holiday she may never see him again and she didn't even want to think about that .

She realised she was alone in the cabin . Adam must already be on deck or in the galley . She was about to get out of bed when there was a gentle tap on the door . "Can I come in?" he asked .

"Of course" she replied "it's your boat".

He came in with a tray laden with fruit juice , eggs , bacon , toast and coffee "Thought you might need a big breakfast after all the energy you used up last night" he flashed that remarkable smile of his and his eyes twinkled so softly that her insides melted just looking into them . He then stooped to kiss her tenderly on the lips and she realised at that moment that he was exactly like his grandfather …..a caring and loving person and a real gentleman . She knew how she felt about what had happened last night , she only hoped he was feeling the same .

When they had finished breakfast he took the tray back to the galley . She asked him if it was okay to wash her hair and have a shower , he went to fetch some towels for her . It was only then that she remembered she only had the clothes she had worn yesterday , as she had not expected to stay overnight . She was still wrapped in the towel when she called to Adam , he came immediately .

"Do you think I could borrow one of your tee-shirts please , just for today , as I didn't bring a change of clothes with me".

"Sure" he said and he went to the cabin next door and brought out two very smart ladies tops ,"Here you can borrow one of these".

Vicky took the top one and went back to his cabin to get dressed . She was quite literally devastated that he so casually offered her the women's tops . How many women did he entertain on the boat . She could have cried . She wondered if he said all those beautiful words and performed with all his women as he had with her last night . She finished dressing , and quickly composing herself , she went up on deck . Adam was busy pulling up the anchor and he told her they were almost ready to go back . Last night she had never wanted the night to end , she had felt so special in his arms , now realising she was probably one in a long line of conquests to him , she felt as if she couldn't get away quick enough .

When they were underway she sunbathed on the deck and pretended to be asleep so not a lot of conversation passed between them on the way back .

They soon arrived at the port and tied up . They gathered their things together and went ashore . When they reached the car Adam asked " Are you alright , Doughnut?" .

"Fine" she replied , but she still felt nauseous inside her stomach .

They then got into the car and he drove her back to her apartment in Sandown .

Today was Friday and she was going home tomorrow.

When they arrived he came around and opened the car door for her ,she got out and started to walk towards the house . He caught her hand and swung her around towards him " Hey , you haven't said goodbye yet". he looked into her eyes and he could see that she was trying so hard to hold back the tears "we've still got one night , where would you like to go?"

"Perhaps I could come up to the house this afternoon to say goodbye to your grandfather as I'm leaving very early on the ferry in the morning".

"Shall I pick you up at 2 o'clock then?"

"Don't worry I can drive myself up there . Oh , thank you so much for the boat ride it was lovely".

Lovely! thought Adam , lovely! , it was pretty devastatingly fabulous for me!

He pulled her towards him and gave her such a sensual kiss that it sent soft tingles rippling all through her .

He ended the kiss and said "I'll see you later at the house then".

As he walked back to his car she turned and hurried up the steps to the front door , she could not look back . She found the key , let herself in and shut the door quickly and was sobbing loudly as she hurried to her apartment door . Once inside she ran to the bedroom and flung herself down onto the bed and let the tears flow until there were none left . How could she have been so stupid , she was head over heels in love with Adam Moore . Why! oh , why did she have to fall in love with a guy who had no intentions towards her whatsoever . How was she going to face him this afternoon . She went into the bathroom and splashed water over her face and buried her head in a soft towel , then looked into the mirror . Her eyes were red and swollen….she couldn't go looking like this….unless she feigned a cold coming on . Yes , that's what she would say to Harry if he made any comment .

She sorted through her clothes and packed what she could into her suitcase then sat on the bed running over in her mind everything that had happened in the last two weeks . Seeing the house , meeting Harry , those wonderful days with Adam….well better to have loved and lost than never loved at all , she thought.

Vicky drove up to the house and parked her car . She knocked on the back door and Diana , Adam's mother came to answer it . She was lovely , quite tall , well taller than Vicky and she had on a very stylish dress . She had very thick blonde hair and it looked as if she had just returned from the hairdressers . She wore very little make-up and was extremely attractive for her age . According to Harry's story she was born in 1948 so that would make her 59 years old , but she looked much younger .

"Oh , you must be Vicky , I'm so pleased to meet you" she held out her hand to shake Vicky's . "We only arrived back from our holiday late on Wednesday , do come in".

What a charming lady , Vicky thought . "I just came to say goodbye to Harry as I'm going back to the mainland tomorrow".

"Father's in his usual place in the garden next door" said Diana .

Vicky enquired as to whether Adam was there .

"No" answered Diana "he's had to pop out for a while , he'll be back later".

"Oh , I wondered if you could give him this top he lent to me". She held out the ladies top that she had rinsed , dried and ironed before she came .

"Thank you" said Diana "Oh! It's one of mine that I leave on his boat in case I go on a trip and need to change , good thing we're about the same size".

Vicky's mouth dropped open "Oh! I thought perhaps it belonged to one of his girlfriends".

"No" said his mother "Adam had a bad experience with a girl a few years ago and he hasn't had a girlfriend since then . He's thrown himself into his work and says he hasn't had time for the ladies.....although he did tell me earlier that this last two weeks spent with you and my father had been his happiest in years . Well I must get the kettle on , could you please tell Father that I'll come and fetch him for his tea in a little while . He'll love seeing you , he's talked of nothing else since we got back".

As Vicky walked over to the garden next door she mulled over what Diana had said about her son and she felt a little guilty for thinking that Adam entertained many women on the boat . As she approached Harry she heard him say "Is that you Sarah?".

"No , Harry , it's me Vicky".

"Oh! I 'm so pleased to see you , my dear , I must have been dreaming" he mused to himself "I thought I saw Sarah walking towards me".

Vicky sat down in the empty deckchair beside Harry and felt the need to hold his hand .

"Harry" she said sadly "I'm going home tomorrow and I wanted to come to tell you how much I have enjoyed myself with you and Adam these past two weeks , it's been the best holiday I've ever had and the most fascinating as well". Emotion was welling up inside of her.

Harry looked up at her and smiled "I'm so glad you came too , it was fate , it was meant to be , just like Sarah and me".

Vicky laughed "Go on with you . I think you're a little too old for me don't you , Harry?".

He winked at her and said "I think you know exactly what I mean Vicky", and with that he squeezed her hand and closed his eyes for a moment .

Before long Diana came to call them for tea .

"I must be going" said Vicky .

"Not until after tea" piped up Harry "besides you haven't said goodbye to Adam yet , have you?"

"Alright then" she then helped Harry up from his deckchair and they walked slowly towards the house .

They sat on the patio at the back of the house overlooking the beautiful garden . They ate freshly made sandwiches and fruit cake and Diana was just pouring the tea when the phone rang . She put the teapot down and went to answer it .

"Vicky , it's Adam for you , dear" and with that she handed the cordless phone to Vicky .

Vicky excused herself and left the patio and walked down the garden path . "Hello".

"Hi! Doughnut , I'm so sorry that I haven't got back for tea" he sounded apologetic "only

something cropped up".

I wonder what , thought Vicky accusingly , and then she was cross with herself for her jealous thoughts .

"Could we go out to dinner tonight?"

"That would be nice".

"I'll pick you up at your apartment at 7 o'clock … alright?"

"I'll see you at seven then" then she hung up . She was half excited and half sad .

She walked back to the patio and saw that Diana was helping Harry out of his chair .

"Father would like to see you in his sitting room…. alone" Diana said with a wink and a smile .

So Vicky helped Harry through to his room and she sat him down near the long window , where he had a superb view of the sea . "Could you pass me that little brown chest from the sideboard , please , my dear".

Vicky went over to the sideboard , picked up the box and brought it back to Harry . He very carefully opened it and reached in and he brought out an exquisitely engraved gold locket and he opened it . Inside was a picture of Harry on one side and another of Sarah on the other . He handed it to Vicky .

"It's beautiful" said Vicky , it almost took her breath away as she took it to look at the pictures.

"I want you to have it" beamed Harry .

"Oh no! I couldn't possibly take it , it's a family heirloom".

"Exactly" agreed Harry "When you marry and have a daughter you can pass it down to her".

Vicky felt very honoured that Harry wanted her to have such a wonderous thing but she couldn't take it .

At that moment Diana knocked and came into the room "Okay , you two?" she said smiling and Vicky sensed she knew something was afoot .

"Harry wants me to have this locket but I don't feel it's right".

"If Father wants you to have it , you take it dear".

"But it's a family heirloom , you or your sister should have it". Vicky held it out to Diana.

Diana smiled as she took the locket from Vicky and looked lovingly inside at the pictures of her mother and father , she closed it and pressed it back into Vicky's hand . "Enjoy wearing it , my dear , better on you than sitting in a box on Father's sideboard".

"Are you really sure?" sighed Vicky still looking fondly at the locket and Diana nodded her approval .

Vicky knelt on the floor in front of Harry's chair and held his hand . "Thank you so much Harry , it's a marvellous momento of my wonderful holiday , especially meeting you and hearing all about Sarah . I shall always cherish it and wear it every day and think of you" she had tears in her eyes . "Now , I have to go because I am seeing Adam tonight , he is taking me out to dinner to say goodbye" she kissed Harry on his cheek and went to say goodbye to Diana . Harry watched her go and said to himself aloud "I think you mean au-revoir , Vicky , not goodbye". he smiled to himself and settled back contentedly into his armchair and looked out towards the sea .

Vicky took great care over her appearance as she showered and dressed . She really wanted to look extra special this evening . She had chosen a little black dress , plain but very stylish , short but very sexy . She put on a pair of black sling-back shoes with a little diamante decoration on the front and , of course , she wore the gold locket that Harry had given her earlier . In case it turned cold later she thought it would be sensible to take her fluffy , but warm , little black jacket with her . Although she was feeling very sad tonight because this could be her last night with Adam she hoped she didn't look as if she was going to a funeral with all the black she was wearing .

She was ready to leave when Adam arrived at 7 pm . When she opened the front door he was waiting on the steps ."You look very lovely tonight" he was looking her up and down with a very approving eye .

"Thank you" said Vicky re-assured that her earlier effort to look good was well worth it .

They walked to a renowned local restaurant and had a superb meal and afterwards Adam suggested they go for a walk along the seafront . He held her hand and they walked in silence for a while , taking in the sight of the moonlight shining on the sea . He then stopped by the railings at a very secluded spot and pulled her into his arms and just gazed into her eyes for what seemed a very long time . "Thank you for eating half of my chocolate bar" he murmured softly "and for biting my cream doughnut ......thank you for finding my Grandfather and me.....thank you for all the wonderful times we've spent together in the last two weeks".

Vicky didn't know whether to laugh or cry "You're welcome" she said as she turned to lean on the railings and look out over the water . "I've had a wonderful time too , you know", she couldn't look at him for a moment frightened that she would let herself down by crying .

He then wrapped his arms all around her and nuzzled into her neck and whispered in her ear . "Stay" he said in a gentle yet provocative tone .

She turned herself within his arms and looked up at him with a puzzled look on her face .

"Stay a little longer" he purred , she was looking up into his big warm brown eyes and her heart was melting with love . He then lowered his lips to hers and ardently embarked on a marathon kiss .She pulled out of the kiss and her eyes darted away quickly and she turned to look back towards the sea ."My ferry leaves at 9 am in the morning and I have to get back for the business and Snowy". What is wrong with me , she thought , this fabulous guy has just asked me to stay and I have to get back for a budgie . Then she said "Why don't we go back to my place for coffee and you can stay a while and we can talk".

I won't be doing much talking , thought Adam , looking down at her beautiful curls , sweet little face and amazingly voluptuous figure in that little black dress .

Didn't she realise how he felt about her , hang on , how did he feel about her? He didn't want to be hurt again and perhaps she thought that this was just a holiday romance . Was he doing the right thing by asking her to stay anyway?

He took her hand in his and they walked back to the apartment and at the door he said

" Maybe I should say goodbye here".

"No , please" pleaded Vicky "please come in".

He didn't need much persuasion , so they went in .

Vicky brought the coffee into the lounge on a tray and they sat opposite one another , her on the small settee and him in a chair .

"Now we're here I can't think of anything to talk about" she grinned and sounded a little nervous "except to say that I've had a most wonderful holiday and I really don't want to go home even though I know I must". she tried to force a sweet smile "meeting Harry and hearing all about your grandparents was fascinating and I shall always remember our time together".

He rose from the chair and came towards her holding out both of his hands , she took them and he pulled her up from the settee into his arms . He held her so close and then running his fingers through her hair and looking lovingly into her eyes he lowered his mouth to hers and she felt as if she was seeing stars as he kissed her . The kiss seemed endless , then he raised his head , looked almost earnestly at her and nodded towards the bedroom "Would you mind" he asked . Ever the gentleman , she thought , and she shook her head knowing that she was aching for him to hold her close and touch her again . He lifted her and carried her to the bedroom and as they undressed each other and laid on the bed Vicky knew she was about to embark on another night of unbridled passion .

The alarm startled her at 7 am . She had set it before she went out with Adam the previous evening , because she knew that if he came back to the apartment the last thing on her mind would be an alarm clock .

Her thoughts strayed to the night of passion they had just shared . He had made her feel as if she would dissolved into liquid with his kisses . His lips had made an intimate journey all over her naked body . His arms had held her so close she felt as if they were as one.... and then they were as one as he'd penetrated her most thoroughly and she knew they were made to be together forever . Oh , how lucky she was to have found Adam . Harry had been right all along , fate had played it's part in the making of all this .

Adam , where was he , perhaps he was making the coffee in the kitchen . She got up itching to kiss him again and hold him close . She went into the kitchen but he wasn't there . She searched the apartment , he was nowhere , and then she found the note on the table .....Bye...thanks for everything...love Adam .

"Bye" her inside felt sick and she found herself screaming loudly "Thanks for everything , Love Adam" How could he do this to her especially after all they had shared last night . If he had really loved her he wouldn't have just gone

"Oh no!" she didn't know how she was going to get through this . She was now feeling totally hysterical inside , she also felt a fool , falling in love so hard and everything ending like this . She suddenly wanted to get into her car and go to his parent's house and confront him but what good would that do . She didn't want to give him the satisfaction of knowing how much he had hurt her . After all he had never told her that he loved her , nor she him , so she would just have to put it down to experience and try so hard to forget him and never let it happen again . The tears were falling down her face as she realised she had said all this before , but Adam , he was different to all the others . She had never fallen so deeply in love before and now he was gone .

She felt so sick she couldn't eat any breakfast , so she showered , dressed , finished her packing and was ready to leave by 8 am . She had to be at the ferry terminal at 8-30 am .

She placed all of her luggage into her little car and left the keys in the designated box . She sighed heavily as she left and drove towards Cowes and the journey home , trying all the time to stem the flow of inevitable tears .

On the ferry she stood at the back of the ship and as the ferry sailed passed the harbour she saw the Lady Eleanor moored by the quay and she was left gazing back at the island thinking of all the sweet and tender memories she would be taking home with her .

Tears started to fall again and she couldn't stop them from streaming down her face . She watched until it all disappeared from sight . She reflected on her holiday once more and thought how quickly the two weeks had flown and she decided that when she left the ferry and returned to the mainland she would forget that the last fortnight had ever happened , but then she put her hand to her throat and felt Harry and Sarah's locket and she knew she would never ever be able to forget all that had happened on her trip to the island .

On the journey home she stopped at a supermarket to buy some bread and milk and a few other essentials and looking towards the coffee shop her thoughts drifted back as she remembered what had happened in the other supermarket just two weeks before . Was she ever going to be able to forget .

Chapter 6.

VICKY arrived home at midday and found that her brother had dropped Snowy off earlier . He had left a note saying that he didn't want her to come home to an empty house after her holiday , she appreciated that . The little white bird cheeped and cheeped as she opened the door of his cage . He came straight out and jumped onto her hand and was saying "kiss…kiss" . she kissed the little bird and said "Well , at least you still love me Snowy". Then the tears promptly started flowing down her cheeks again , surely everything she said and did wasn't going to remind her of Adam was it?

She made herself a drink and a sandwich and sat down to try to relax after her long drive .

She looked around her lounge and realised she was quite glad to be back home in familiar surroundings . She had bought this house about four years before . She was lucky enough to have inherited quite a substantial sum of money from her maternal grandmother whom she had adored . She was so grateful that Granny had thought of her and she realised that putting the money into property was probably the best thing she had ever done . As she didn't have a mortgage now it meant she could be self-employed without having to worry if she had a few lean weeks with her business at times . The house had three fair sized bedrooms and a bathroom upstairs which was very handy if she ever had guests who needed to stay over . Then downstairs there was a lounge , a large kitchen-diner , a small sewing room and at the side of the house a considerably large extension housing the fancy dress with an extra loo which was handy for her customers as well as herself . She felt very fortunate and secure somehow . In the comfort of her little home she felt she was away from all the sadness and unhappiness in the outside world . Who was she kidding , she had brought some of it home with her and she knew she would have to pull herself out of this if she was going to get over him .

She had finished her snack now and thought it may be a good idea to unpack her case and start the washing . That was the only drawback arriving home from holiday....all the washing . She was busy putting her mug and plate into the kitchen sink when the phone rang . Her heart jumped in her chest , could that possibly be Adam she wondered as she slowly picked up the receiver and very tentatively said "Hello".

"Is that the fancy dress hire?" a ladies voice was on the other end .

"Yes" answered Vicky .

"I'd like to make an appointment to come over as I have a party tonight . I hope it's not too short notice , only I've been ringing all week and I couldn't get hold of you".

"Oh , I am sorry about that I've been away on holiday for a while and I've only just got back . I'll fetch the diary and take down your details, just a moment". Coming back to the phone Vicky asked "What name is it?"

"Wanda James" said the lady .

"Will 5 o'clock suit you" Vicky enquired .

"That will be fine , see you then" said Wanda and she hung up . As she hadn't asked for directions Vicky presumed she had been before . She then thought to herself that it didn't seem as if she had been away .

After replacing the phone in the holder she decided to open her mail . There were a few bills and a couple of welcome invitations . One was a retirement party for an ex-colleague Mary , at the office where she worked before she went self-employed . They had kept in touch and Mary always invited her to all the outings and social activities etc: This one was on the 16th of June , that's only three weeks away , she thought . The other invitation was to a cheese and wine evening at a friend's home in the village in aid of the local church heating fund . She found her diary and put the dates in and then she thought she would write the acceptance replies as soon as possible before she forgot .

She smiled to herself as she realised that neither of the invites was fancy dress . She was still laughing to herself thinking she couldn't remember the last time she had been to a fancy dress party when the phone rang again . This time it was her mum .

"Did you have a lovely holiday?" she asked .

Vicky chatted to her mother about her holiday in general and after a while she excused herself on the pretence that having only just got home she needed to go to the loo .

"Well don't forget you're here for lunch tomorrow , you can tell us all about it then , bye love" her mum rang off .

Vicky's eyes were a little teary "How am I going to cope with talking about it" she cried loudly "when all I'm doing is trying so hard to forget".

She went back to her correspondence . She picked up the retirement invitation to reply and noticed that it had a PS at the bottom saying that it would be a Hollywood Red Carpet theme , adding that she and her partner could dress as glamorous as they liked . Well at least I can dress in something really fantastic , she thought , trying to take her mind off of Adam . Then it occurred to her that she had no-one to go with and she suddenly felt quite lonely again .

She was day-dreaming about walking down the red carpet with Adam at her side when once again the sound of the phone brought her back to the present .

"Hi! Vicky , darling" it was her best friend Liz. They had been at senior school together and had stayed in touch all these years .Liz was someone who could brighten up a room as soon as she walked into it . She was a bubbly blonde with quite a rounded figure which suited her personality perfectly . She was married but as yet had no family . She was quite the career girl , a nurse in a local G P's practise and she and Vicky got together as often as possible . Liz and her husband , Brian , had also been away on holiday to Spain for the last fortnight , so they hadn't spoken since before Vicky went away .

"How was the holiday!" asked Liz "I can't wait to hear all about it". She sounded excited

"Oh it was okay".

"Okay , okay is that all?"

"No , I really had a nice time" Vicky sounded far too sullen .

"Look don't try to pull the wool over my eyes , Vicks , I've known you for too long . What happened , come on out with it".

"Oh , Liz" cried Vicky , tears starting to roll down her face and then without taking a breath she let it all out . "I went to the supermarket and I met this gorgeous man , I ate his chocolate bar , took a bite out of his doughnut , met this lovely old man and after hearing his life story I met the gorgeous man again , sprained my ankle , then had some marvellous times with him , fell in love with him and we made fantastic love together and then he left me without saying goodbye and now I'm so miserable . Oh , Liz whatever am I going to do?" by now she was sobbing .

Liz was stunned into silence .

"Liz , are you still there?"

"Yes" stuttered Liz "hang on I'm coming over , put the kettle on and I'll be there as soon as I can".

Vicky hung up then took her handkerchief from her bag and buried her head in it and cried and cried until her tear-ducks were dry . But she did feel slightly better getting it all off her chest .

Liz arrived about 15 minutes later and gave Vicky a super hug . "You look awful".

"Oh , thanks" said Vicky as she made the tea .

They went to the lounge and sat down .

"What a rat" fumed Liz "I'll kill him if I ever get hold of him" .

"Oh , no Liz , Adam wasn't like that at all".

"Well why are you in such a state then?"

"I'm just so in love with him at the moment , I'm going to have to work hard trying to get over him , please give me a little time" pleaded Vicky .

"Right I want to know everything from the beginning to the end , and don't leave anything out!".

Vicky poured everything out , well almost everything , and she was so glad she had such a super friend to confide in .

"Didn't he even give you his phone number?" Liz enquired at the end of the saga .

"Oh , yes" said Vicky "I had forgotten that , I have a business card in my bag , but I'm not going to ring him , my pride wouldn't let me , after all it was him who dumped me".

"Have you got any appointments today?".

"Just one , a lady coming at 5 pm"

"Right , after you've seen to her , get your glad rags on and we'll go out to the pub tonight and drown our sorrows . I've had a little spat with Brian today and I could do with a little female company myself . Oh men" Liz said with a smile "who'd have them".

Vicky laughed , Liz did cheer her up somewhat . "You haven't told me about your holiday yet"

"We'll talk about it tonight , I'll pick you up at 8 o'clock" Liz said as she left .

Vicky would look forward to that , at least it may take her mind off of a certain man she was sure she would never be able to forget completely .

A couple of weeks went by and she tried to keep herself busy catching up on sewing jobs etc: and she felt she was almost winning the battle . Things kept cropping up to remind her , like the little sand bottle , a momento from their trip to Alum Bay and the set of coffee mugs . She loved them and wanted to use them but each time she drank her coffee from them her mind wandered back to the little café and the magical house and Harry . She felt awful that she hadn't rung Harry since she got back . After all it wasn't his fault that Adam had dumped her .

It was Saturday , usually her busiest day , the phone rang and she picked it up and cheerily said "Fancy Dress Hire". she heard a gentleman ask if he could make an appointment . The phone line was a bit crackly . She asked if 4 o'clock would be okay.

"Fine" he replied and then just as she asked his name the phone cut off . Must have been a mobile in a bad signal area , she thought as she jotted it down in the diary.

Later whilst she was talking on the phone to Bill , the manager of the local shopping centre in the town nearby , with reference to the costumes she would be making for this years Christmas grotto , she heard the doorbell . "Bill , I'll have to ring you back on Monday and arrange to pop in to see you , only my 4 o'clock appointment has just arrived so I must go". She quickly replaced the receiver and hurried to answer the door .

She opened the door , looked up and her mouth dropped open .

"Hello , Doughnut" he said with a cheeky smile .

Without thinking Vicky just flung herself at him , she put her arms around his neck and kissed him squarely on the lips .

"You're pleased to see me then?" he said .

"I could kill you , Adam Moore" she said pulling away , "you left me without saying goodbye" by now tears were running down her cheeks and she could do nothing to stop them .

He'd never seen her like this "Don't cry , Doughnut" he said softly , pulling her towards him once more ."please can I come in ?"

She suddenly realised they were still on the doorstep so she let him in and shut the door .

They walked through to the kitchen and she put the kettle on to make a drink . "Coffee or tea" she asked .

"Tea please" answered Adam "and you wouldn't happen to have a kit-kat to go with it would you?" he smiled .

She laughed to herself , he would never let her forget that , she thought . "Sorry no , but I do have some home-made cookies if you would like one", she went to the pantry reached for the biscuit container and placed some on a plate .

They walked through to her lounge and sat side by side on the settee . Adam took a biscuit and ate it ."Well you certainly know the way to a man's heart".

Vicky looked hurt .

"What's the matter , Doughnut?" he asked .

"Talking about hearts you certainly know how to break one".

"Vicky" he said gently .

"You will never know how much you hurt me"

"Vicky" he said softly again .

"You will never know how wretched I felt"

"Vicky" , he said again but she wasn't listening to him , she was so full of self-pity.

"When you left that morning you broke my heart into a million pieces".

"Vicky" he said louder .

"Yes". Thank goodness she'd heard him .

"Vicky" he whispered softly "will you please let me put those pieces back together again?"

She just crumpled into his arms and he pulled her towards him and kissed her with a passion that could only be shared by two people who were meant for each other .

He pulled away looking deeply and lovingly into her eyes ."Marry me?" he asked tenderly

She was just so stunned she couldn't speak and as the tears started to flow again she muttered something inaudible .

"I hope that was a yes?"

She nodded and returned his kiss never wanting it to end .

Adam ended the kiss and reached into his pocket and withdrew quite an old box . He opened the box to reveal a sparkling ruby ring in the shape of a flower . "It was my grandmother's engagement ring . Grandfather gave it to me and he said if you said 'yes' he would like you to have it".

Vicky was completely overcome . When she looked at the ring she realised it was shaped like a daisy and she remembered that Harry had told her about the real daisy ring he had given to Sarah when he had proposed to her.

"It's so beautiful" she smiled radiantly.

"Just like you" he beamed "and I love you so very much". He took her left hand in his and placed the ruby ring onto her third finger , it was a perfect fit .

Vicky had never felt so blissfully happy in all her life "and I love you too" she replied .

He was still holding her hand when he said "I think I owe you an explanation" and he went on to tell her that when he woke up on that last morning he just couldn't say goodbye to her as it would have been too painful . He wasn't at all sure that Vicky was serious about the relationship and had taken the cowards way out which wasn't normally like him at all . Over the last two weeks he had moped about and had been thoroughly miserable and his grandfather had noticed .

One day when he went into the garden to fetch his grandfather for his tea Harry had asked him to sit down for a little chat . "What is it , son?" he asked Adam .

"Nothing Grandfather , I'm fine". his reply had not been very convincing .

"Nothing gets passed me , Adam" said Harry "it's Vicky isn't it?"

"Yes , Grandfather , I miss her so much , I never knew my heart could ache like this . I didn't think I would ever fall in love again after Megan".

Adam had met Megan when he had gone to an advertising conference in Cardiff . She was the event organiser and they had hit it off immediately and had become lovers . The affair had lasted for three years . They had never lived together because their jobs meant that they moved around quite a lot   But the nature of her job meant that she met lots of different people and Megan had fallen for one of her clients and Adam had been devastated at the time . He realised now that the way he felt about Vicky meant that he hadn't really loved Megan at all .

"What shall I do , Grandfather ?"

"What do you want to do , my son?"

"I want to find her and tell her how much I love her , but I don't know how she feels about me".

"Well I know exactly how she feels , son" exclaimed Harry "every time she spoke to me about you her eyes lit up like diamonds and I've only ever seen that look once before in a woman and that was your grandmother . I remember how she looked at me when I asked her to marry me . You mustn't let Vicky go , my son , do you know how to contact her?"

"She gave me a business card when she was here , I could ring her".

"No , son" advised Harry "you must go to see her personally , but first take me into the house to my sitting room".

Adam did as his grandfather asked and when they reached the sitting room Harry asked him to pass the little brown chest from the sideboard to him . He had then produced the engagement ring that he had given to Sarah all those years ago . " I want you to give this to Vicky if she agrees to marry you . Good Luck , son , and make sure you let me know when you find her".

Adam had caught the next available ferry to the mainland and had phoned Vicky from his mobile to make the 4 o'clock appointment .

Coming back to the present Vicky kissed Adam softly . " I thought you had rung from a mobile phone because you lost the signal half way through the call".

"No , I hung up because I wanted to surprise you and I was afraid you wouldn't want to see me if you knew who it was". He enfolded her in his arms and drew her closer to him . "Vicky , I love you more than words can say and I know that I want to spend the rest of my life with you".

"How could you ever think that I would never want to see you again after all we had shared . No-one has ever made me feel as wanted and desired as you do and I never loved anyone before in my life as I love you now".

"Oh , Vicky , you've made me the happiest man in the world, and now would you please talk to my grandfather".

"Whatever for?"

"Because he is so worried about us and he asked me to let him know when I found you . I thought you may like to tell him that you've accepted my proposal".

Adam tapped in his mother's phone number and passed the mobile phone to Vicky . Harry answered .

"Hello Harry it's Vicky".

"Well how wonderful to hear from you my dear , how are you?"

"I'm feeling absolutely marvellous" she replied " and I'm ringing to invite you to a wedding".

Harry smiled to himself as he asked "Anyone I know?"

Vicky passed the phone back to Adam "She said yes , Grandfather". Harry could almost feel the happiness coming through the phone and he felt elated .

"I'm so happy for you both and I can't wait to see you together again , don't leave it too long before you come to see me" . Then Harry hung up .

Adam asked her if there was anyone else she would like to share the news with , lucky for Vicky she had no more appointments that day .

"The only thing I want to share is the next few hours with you , showing you how much I love you".

Adam was more than happy to oblige and was suddenly consumed with a hunger for Vicky that he had never felt before.

They made their way to her bedroom and they closed the door on the world outside knowing that the love they had for each other was all they needed to create a magical world of their very own .

The next morning as they sat having breakfast together they made plans for the next few months . They would put Vicky's business on the market , although she would obviously carry on as usual until it was sold . They would get married on the island and live in Adam's house in Southampton . They were so very happy .

Adam had to travel back to Southampton that day because he had some important business to attend to first thing on Monday morning . So later that day after he had left , assuring her that he would ring he as soon as he got back , Vicky rang her mum . She had already arranged to go to her parents house for Sunday lunch that day so she told her mum that she had something to tell them . She didn't want to tell her mum on the phone , she wanted to tell her mum and dad together .

When Adam got home that day he rang her to tell her that he had arrived back safely . She had forgotten to ask him if he would come with her to the Hollywood Red Carpet retirement party the next Saturday . She explained the theme of the party and asked if he would like to accompany her .

"Of course I'll come , I would be delighted to take you anywhere".

She was so excited " It's this coming Saturday the 16th of June, are you free?"

"I'll make sure I am" and he immediately made a note of it in his dairy and told her he would ring her in the week to arrange the time etc:

She told him she was about to leave to have lunch with her parents and to tell them the good news .

He blew a kiss over the phone and said "See you on Saturday then , oh , and Doughnut" he purred "I love you" he really did sound like the cat who got the cream .

"I love you too , my darling" she replied feeling so warm ,so safe and so in love .

They hung up .

There was just one person that Vicky was aching to tell and she couldn't resist picking up the phone immediately after she had spoken to Adam .

"Hello" her best friend answered the call .

"Liz , it's Vicky."

"Hello , sweetie , how are you coping?". She sounded very sympathetic and was fully expecting Vicky to want to cry on her shoulder once again .

"Oh! Liz", Vicky was almost in tears but not sad ones " the most amazing thing has happened , you are not going to believe it but Adam came to see me yesterday afternoon , oh , Liz it was wonderful"

"Well I hope the cad isn't leading you up the garden path . He'll have me to deal with if he hurts you again" she sounded as if she was on the warpath .

"No , Liz , he has asked me to marry him , I've accepted and now we're engaged".

Liz didn't know whether she was pleased for her friend or not . She had spent the last two weeks listening patiently whilst Vicky had reminisced about the high and low points of her holiday and her relationship with Adam and she didn't want Vicky going through all that again if this guy changed his mind once more . "Oh , Vicks , I hope you know what you are doing and anyway why did it take you this long to ring me and tell me about it?".

"Well he stayed the night and he's not long left . I know I'm doing the right thing Liz and I hope you're happy for me".

" I am happy for you , sweetie , but I hope he doesn't let you down again , I've hated seeing you so sad the last two weeks . Why don't you pop around and we'll have a natter over a cuppa"

"Well I'm just off to have lunch with my parents and to tell them about Adam , I'll call in to see you on the way back".

"I'll look forward to that , bye sweetie" Liz rang off .

Vicky sat in the armchair and wrapped her arms around herself , almost cuddling herself , she had never felt more contented with her life than she did now .

Chapter 7.

SATURDAY 16th of June arrived and Vicky was so looking forward to this evening . It was the night of the 'Hollywood Red Carpet' retirement party .

She had quite a few appointments through until lunchtime but she had left the afternoon free so that she could go to get her hair done at 2 o'clock .

Adam had rung to say he would arrive at approximately 4 o'clock and she was so excited at the thought of seeing him again . He was so fabulously handsome and her heart flipped every time she thought about him .

After all her clients had gone she made herself a light lunch of cottage cheese , crackers, and fruit juice although she really didn't know how she was going to eat it because she felt too excited and nervous about tonight .

All her old colleagues would be there and she was going to show off her new man . She had butterflies in her stomach already or was that the anticipation of seeing Adam again . She hadn't felt like this for a long time and had almost forgotten what it was like to be in love but she was quite happily getting used to it again .

After she had eaten she got her coat and set out to the hairdressers . She arrived a little early so she browsed through the jewellers shop next door . She saw a very smart pair of cufflinks and a tie pin set which she thought Adam might like and she decided to buy them . Then she realised that she didn't even know when his birthday was , not that it mattered . Her mind then wandered to the fact that although they had talked a lot in the few weeks since they had met , they actually didn't know that much about one another , then she smiled to herself thinking , well we have the rest of our lives to find out . She bought the set and the assistant gift wrapped it , which she thought was a very nice touch .

She then made her way to the hairdressers . She had her hair put up at the back with just a few wisps down in front of her ears . She also had a manicure and her nails painted .

She was going to be wearing a long dress which she had bought in Macey's in America when she was on holiday there . It was in a dark pink sparkly material which seemed to change colour as you moved in the light . She would borrow some jewellery from the fancy dress drawer which was all glittery and looked like diamonds and she had a very smart pair of silver shoes which would match nicely . She also had a silver evening bag and a stole . She almost felt as if she was going in fancy dress .

She arrived home at 3-30 pm to find Adam waiting outside in his car . She apologised...

"No need , I'm early" he said , getting out of his car and pulling her into his arms and into the most passionate of kisses .

She sighed contentedly as it ended .

"Did you miss me , my darling Doughnut" he asked smiling .

"You will never know how much" she replied embarking on another one of their marathon kisses and feeling the warmth of his passion searing right through her .

Adam eventually pulled away and remarked "Well your neighbours will certainly have something to talk about if we stay out here much longer".

They both laughed and she unlocked the door and they went inside .

"I'm going to have to give you the spare key , I don't like the thought of you having to wait outside in your car".

"You're so thoughtful , Doughnut , the key to your door , the final seal of approval on our relationship is it?" he laughed , but Vicky looked quite seriously at him .

"Adam , you are serious about us aren't you?" she looked really worried .

"Oh , Doughnut , of course I am , I was only joking . Sorry Darling , come here". He pulled her into his arms and held her closely hoping that the ensuing kiss would convince her .

Vicky was still very nervous about their relationship after Adam had walked out on her on the island and she still needed re-assuring that it would never happen again.

As he surfaced from the kiss he looked at her and said "Your hair looks gorgeous , by the way , you will be the belle of the ball tonight".

"Thank you".

Adam felt the tension ease a little .

Vicky went through to the kitchen and he followed her as she went to put the kettle on "Coffee okay?"

He nodded then asked "Do you mind if I hang my suit up somewhere?"

"Go into the fancy dress room and hang it on one of the rails".

He did so and was fascinated by all the different costumes that Vicky had either collected or made . She followed him into the room . "If we were going to a fancy dress party who would you like to be?"

"I could be Rhett Butler and you could be my Scarlett O'Hara" he purred in a very sexy voice .

"Or we could be Mickey and Minnie Mouse , I think they loved each other almost as much as we do" she giggled .

Adam took her into his arms and looked deeply into her sparkling grey eyes and said "Nobody loves anyone as much as I love you , my Darling".

Tears of happiness started falling and she mouthed "Thank you" and he kissed her again .

She drew away after a moment and said "Thank you for loving me . You know I will always love you with all my heart , body and soul . I have done ever since we met again in Harry's garden .

"And I realise now that I have loved you since the first day I laid eyes on you in the supermarket restaurant".

They held each other in another embrace and then she reminded him that their coffee was getting cold so they went through to the lounge and he saw that on the plate beside his mug of coffee was a Kit-Kat . He looked at her and laughed .

"Just paying you back" she smiled .

After drinking their coffee Adam could not keep his hands off of his beautiful fiance and they had enough time to show their devotion to one another with some wonderful love-making before showering and getting ready to go out .

As she came into the bedroom where he had just dressed she thought how handsome he looked in his black tuxedo , dress shirt and red bow-tie with matching handkerchief in the pocket of his jacket .

"I don't believe it!" he exclaimed "I've forgotten to pack my cufflinks".

"No problem" she said as she went to her handbag and produced the little package from the jewellers . She handed it to him "I bought these for you this afternoon".

When he opened the package he discovered that his initials were on the cufflinks and tie-pin set and he was overwhelmed that she had thought of him . He rewarded her with another of his devastating kisses.

That was worth every penny I spent , she thought as she wallowed in the kiss .

"I only have to put my dress and jewellery on and then I'm ready" she had already tidied her hair , which had become a little dishevelled as a result of their love-making and she had re-applied her make-up in the bathroom .

When she was dressed she came downstairs into the lounge , where he was waiting , and as she entered the room his mouth fell open ."Oh Doughnut! You look absolutely ravishing , I am the luckiest man in the world to have you . I would kiss you again but I don't want to spoil your make-up , I'll make it up to you later".

"Thank you , I think you look pretty special as well".

Vicky said goodbye to Snowy and left the light and the television on for him . "I don't want him to get lonely while we are out" she laughed .

Vicky locked the front door whilst Adam unlocked the car . He held the passenger door open for her then he got in and asked her to navigate as he had no idea where they were going .

They arrived at the hotel and parked the car and Vicky felt a million dollars in her outfit and the most fortunate girl in the world with Adam holding her arm as they walked up the red carpet to the door . The photographer took some lovely shots and Vicky was thrilled that in years to come they would have a photographic record to look back on of their first night out as an engaged couple . She looked lovingly at him as the snaps were taken and thought to herself , you are my knight in shining armour , my champion , my perfect gentleman , my number one man , my Adam . Then she realised that soon she would be Mrs Adam Moore .

She saw the envious looks of her friends at the party and was very proud to show off her man . Then the music started and he swept her onto the dance floor . They waltzed across the room looking deeply into each other's eyes as if they were the only couple there .

Vicky had never danced so much or laughed so much or ate so much in ages , she was blissfully happy and she and Adam thoroughly enjoyed every moment of it .

Well after midnight , after all the goodbyes had been said , they started back to the car park . On the way Adam suggested that they book into the hotel overnight . Although she very much wanted to say yes , she remembered her little bird . She couldn't ring her neighbour to ask her to pop in and cover the bird and to turn the television off because it was too late . Adam seemed a little cross about it but then he realised that one of the reasoned he loved her so much was because she had such a compassionate nature and she felt a tremendous responsibility towards her little pet .

As he had had quite a lot to drink and she hadn't , she offered to drive home . She hardly ever drank alcohol but only because she didn't like the taste of it . They reached Adam's car and she began to feel slightly nervous about driving a large BMW after only being used to her little VW but she soon got used to it and actually enjoyed the drive home .

They arrived at her house at about 1 am and quietly let themselves in , they put the bird to bed , turned the television off and went through to the kitchen to make a drink .

Suddenly he pulled her into his arms and said "Forget the coffee , you have something that I would love more". With that he started to kiss her all over and as they made their way upstairs they left a trail of clothes behind them.

As they reached her bedroom Adam picked her up and carried her across to the bed laid her down gently then proceeded to make passionate love to her for hours.

In the morning Vicky woke and seeing Adam beside asleep beside her she realised that this was not one of her erotic dreams but the real thing . She would always treasure every moment they spent together and remembering all that had happened the night before she knew she desired him more that she had anyone in her life before . She had never been happier . With a contented sigh she snuggled up to her adorable lover , he stirred , and his hands and his lips began the heavenly journey from the luscious curls on her head to the luscious curls at the other end of her beautiful body and she knew she was in for another brilliant love-making session .

Today Vicky had arranged that they both go to her parent's house for Sunday lunch so that her mum and dad could meet Adam . They lived a couple of miles away and she saw them quite regularly . Usually her mum , Grace , insisted that Vicky join them every Sunday for lunch if she could manage it . Quite often one or both of her brothers and their families would join them .

Jack , her older brother was 32 years old and he was a carpenter . He was married to his childhood sweetheart Sally . They lived in the town nearby and had two lovely children , Christopher aged 7 and Evie who had just celebrated her 4th birthday .

David , her other brother was aged 29 and was married to Susan , although everyone called her Suzy . He had met her when they were working together at a local newspaper office . David was now a freelance photographer / reporter for the paper . They had been married for 5 years and had twins , Lisa and Luke , who were almost 2 years old . Vicky adored her nieces and nephews and had always longed for a family of her own.

Her mum worked part-time at the local garden centre in the cafeteria . She really loved it , meeting all different kinds of people . Vicky's dad was in engineering and was the works manager in a local factory .

Vicky and Adam arrived at 12-30 pm for 1 o'clock lunch . After all the introductions they enjoyed a delicious meal and then her mum suggested that she and Vicky go into the kitchen to make the tea and coffee .

Adam was glad of the opportunity to talk to Vicky's dad , Robert . "As you know Vicky and I have decided to get married". Robert nodded but said nothing . "I would have asked you before but I had to make sure Vicky wanted me first".

Robert smiled broadly "I totally approve of my daughter's choice and as far as her mother and I are concerned as long as she's happy we are happy . I can see just by looking at her that she is , so stop worrying about what her mother and I think , it seems we've got a lot of arranging to do".

Adam rose from the sofa and walked over to Robert and shook his hand "Thank you so much" he said feeling very much relieved .

Just at that moment Vicky and her mum came in with the drinks .

Her mum had been so excited when Vicky had eventually confessed all about Adam and couldn't wait to meet him and also help Vicky with her trousseau and all of the wedding arrangements . Of course Robert and herself would have to meet Adam's parents , Diana and James , to discuss everything . There was so much to think about but she was over the moon . Vicky said she would arrange with Adam when his parents could come over to meet her family . That's if it wouldn't be too much for Harry . If it was perhaps her parents could arrange to go to the island .

Robert looked up at his two favourite ladies and suggested that it might be a good idea to invite Adam' parents and Harry to lunch one day soon . So Adam rang his mother on his mobile and made a date that suited them all .

" It won't be too much for Harry will it?" enquired Vicky .

"He will love a day out" Adam assured her .

They decided on   Sunday 1st of July as that was Robert's 56th birthday and he would enjoy celebrating it that way .

That Sunday came around quite quickly . When Vicky got up , she showered and washed her hair . She felt as if she was walking on air all the time and as she went to the wardrobe to decide what to wear that day the phone rang .

"Hi , Doughnut" she could tell by the way he said that , that he was smiling from ear to ear . "Ready for the big day?"

"Not THE big day" she smiled "What time will you arrive?"

"I thought I would bring everyone over in my father's car . It's bigger than mine and seats five comfortably , so we can pick you up on the way . The ferry is at 9 o'clock so we should be with you by 11-30 am . Is that alright?"

"Of course , I'm so looking forward to meeting your father and seeing your mother again . Are you sure Harry's up to the trip?"

"He can't wait to see you again and has talked about nothing else since I told him about it We'll see you later then" . He then added "Love you , Sweetheart".

Vicky's heart leapt in her chest . Every time he told her he loved her she felt herself sigh with contentment and felt so lucky that he loved her ."I love you too , my darling" she sighed again . "Oh , Adam I can't wait until the real Big Day and then we can be together forever . I've missed you so much".

She hadn't seen him for two weeks and had missed his gentle caresses and tender heart-stopping kisses .

"Only a few more hours and we'll be together again" he sighed "see you soon . Sweetheart I must go , I've got a ferry to catch" he chuckled as he rang off .

She went over to the wardrobe and took out a very pretty cheesecloth dress which had a swirling almost oriental pattern all over it , she felt very summery and surprisingly cool . The weather forecast for today had said it would be very hot . She stooped to get her sandals from the bottom of the wardrobe and felt a slight twinge in her ankle . It was still very tender at times yet it must be over 6 weeks since she hurt it , so she thought it best to steer clear of any high heels for the time being .

She went downstairs after making her bed and tidying her bedroom to have breakfast . She was very nervous about today so she didn't feel very hungry but she went to the fridge to get some yoghurt and bread . She kept the bread in the fridge in the summer , it seemed to keep a little longer . She made herself some toast and she suddenly remembered Snowy . She went through to the lounge and took the cover from his cage and opened the door , he hopped onto her hand and said "Good boy" he talked quite a lot really although she couldn't understand everything he said ."You'll have a new home soon , Snowy" the little budgie chirped as if he had understood what she had said . "Come on let's go and have something to eat". and she took him through to the kitchen with her .

After she had finished her breakfast she tidied the house , although as it was just her and Snowy it didn't get too messed up . It was only the sewing room that was always in a state . When she had finished tidying up she picked up the books of wedding invitation samples to take with her to show her mum and Diana .

She realised that the time had flown as she heard a car stop outside so she went to the door . Adam and his family had arrived , almost on time . Traffic had been quite light at that time of the morning , he said , and only Salisbury was a little busy as they passed through it .

Diana was first out of the car and she came straight to the door to give Vicky a hug . Diana already loved Vicky and the feeling was mutual . James and Adam helped Harry out of the car and Vicky went over to give him a loving cuddle .They went inside and sat Harry in the lounge and before Vicky went to put the kettle on Adam introduced her to his father . James was tall and must have been in his late fifties or early sixties , but he was very handsome for his age , and she could see immediately from whom Adam had inherited his good looks . "I'm so pleased to meet you at last" he said as he shook her hand " and I want you to know how happy we are about you and Adam".

"Not half as happy as I am about it , Father" Adam piped in , at the same time giving her a beaming smile .

"I'm so pleased to meet you too" she answered smiling at James , "Right who's for coffee then?"

Everyone laughed when Harry said " Can I have my usual , tea please".

They all sat down enjoying some of Vicky's home-made biscuits and catching up on all the latest news . Very soon it was 12-30 pm and they decided to make a move to Grace and Robert's because they had a couple of miles to drive and lunch was at 1 pm and they didn't want to be late .

They arrived at the house and went inside and after all the introductions were over , Robert offered everyone pre-lunch drinks . As today was his birthday they gave him some cards and Vicky had a gift for him .

Vicky's parents home was very smart . Detached with a large garden all around it . It had four bedrooms and a bathroom upstairs , but now apart from their own bedroom , the other three were kept for guests . Grace especially loved it when Christopher and Evie came to stay . Although they were a handful for Sally and Jack they always behaved like angels for their Nan . Downstairs there was a large main lounge , a very tastefully decorated dining room , a study and the modern kitchen had recently been extended to incorporate a utility room and extra loo . The house was not as big as Diana and James' but her parents loved it and were very happy there .

"Lunch is ready" called Grace , so everyone went through to the dining room and settled down to eat . Harry was getting quite peckish now . Grace had cooked a superb meal . Mushroom cocktail or soup to start , followed by traditional roast beef with all the trimmings , then homemade apple pie with fresh cream or custard for dessert . Everyone complimented her on such a delicious meal .

Afterwards Harry winked at Adam and said "When you marry a woman you must always look at her mother and I hope Vicky is like her mother , serving up a feast like that" he chuckled . "You will certainly be well looked after , son , but then I knew that as soon as I got to know Vicky".

Adam smiled knowingly at his grandfather and gave Harry an impromptu hug .

When lunch was finished the dishwasher was filled and everything cleared from the table so that Diana , Grace and Vicky could spread the catalogues of wedding invitation samples on the table .

The wedding date had been booked for the 6th of October which gave them almost three months to arrange everything . They had decided to get married on the island because too much travelling wasn't good for Harry and Vicky also loved the church in Shanklin . Adam had booked his yacht clubhouse for the reception and had already booked the honeymoon , a week in Spain , as a surprise for Vicky . She knew they were going away but she didn't know where . They would fly out the day after the wedding .

Vicky called out to Adam who was now sat in the garden with Harry "Would you like to come inside and look at the invitations with us?". She walked over to his chair bent over and planted a kiss on his cheek .

"Whatever you pick , Doughnut , will be fine with me". he then returned hers with another kiss .Vicky returned to the house .

Adam then turned to Harry who had a little tear in his eye . "You alright , Grandfather?"

"Oh , yes" answered Harry "I was just thinking about our wedding , your grandmother's and mine". He sighed heavily "Times have changed so much . We didn't have posh invitations then , but then all that mattered was that we loved one another . You know , son , love is the most important thing in all the world".

"I know Grandfather" replied Adam softly " and I love Vicky more than anything else in the world".

"And she loves you , son , I know . I can see that so plainly when you're both together".

The look of understanding was evident as the two men looked at one another and Adam knew his grandfather had experienced the same feelings with his grandmother all those years ago .

After enjoying a light tea it was time for Adam's family to depart . It was at least an hour and a half drive to the ferry from Vicky's house and they all worried that a long day would be too much for Harry . But he said he was having such a wonderful time he was sorry to be going back so soon .

They all said their goodbye's and the women agreed to meet up the next week to talk about other arrangements and outfits etc: Vicky really wanted her niece , Evie , to be bridesmaid , with her best friend Liz as matron of honour , so their dresses had to be ordered as soon as possible .

When they arrived back at Vicky's house Diana and James said goodbye in the car . Then Vicky got out and went to the passenger door at the back to kiss Harry goodbye and he thanked her for a lovely day .Adam took her to the front door and then stepped inside to say his farewell . They held each other tightly and arranged for Vicky to meet Adam in Southampton the next Saturday.

"I can't wait to see you alone" Vicky was near to tears.

"Don't cry , Doughnut , it tears me up inside when you do . It won't be long and to cheer you up I have booked us into a hotel , so bring an over-night bag . Oh , and please ask your neighbour to baby-sit or should I say bird-sit Snowy . You've got plenty of notice this time". He smiled as he raised his eyes to the ceiling .

She laughed thinking back to the Red Carpet Retirement party when Snowy had taken precedence over him .

"I'm quite jealous of that little chap , he gets all of your attention and gets to kiss you more than I do".

"Well don't worry we'll soon be together every day".

Adam kissed her long and tenderly once more and then said " I must go , we're keeping the others waiting".

How thoughtful of him . "No worries , see you on Saturday and don't forget to ring me when you get home to let me know that you've all got back safely".

"Will do" said Adam as he walked back to the car .

They all waved and Vicky blew a kiss to Harry who , although he was looking very tired returned her gesture with a gorgeous smile . When the car was out of sight she turned and went inside just wishing for the days to fly by until she saw her beloved Adam again on Saturday .

Chapter 8.

VICKY'S mum , Grace , rang the next day to arrange when it would be convenient to go to Bath , Bristol or Salisbury to look at wedding dresses . They chose Tuesday . That would be the best day for Vicky this week because she didn't have any appointments and Grace didn't work at the cafeteria on Tuesdays .

They thought Bath would be a good place to start as it was the closest , so off they went feeling very excited and enthusiastic . The first bridal shop they found was very nice and Vicky tried on some beautiful gowns but she didn't feel quite right in any of them . The second and third shops felt the same , so after a light lunch they trudged off to Bristol .

They visited two shops there and although she looked very lovely in the dresses she had tried on , she knew they weren't exactly what she was looking for .

Then , as they were on their way back to the car park , they found a small shop where the owner made all the gowns herself . As soon as Vicky tried on the first gown she knew it was the one . It had a scooped neck and short sleeves to just above the elbow . The sleeves had tiny shapes cut out in the material that made an open pattern almost like a doily . The whole bodice was patterned with pearls and crystal stones . The front dropped straight down from underneath the bust , and from the waist at the back the dress fanned out into a long train . All around the hem there was a three inch deep border again with pearls and crystals . Best of all it was a perfect fit .

Grace had a tear in her eye as Vicky came out of the changing room . "Oh Vicky , love, you look beautiful". Vicky smiled at her mum and said "Thank you".

As there were no alterations to be made they bought the dress straight away and the dear little lady placed it very carefully into a lovely box . She also gave Vicky a dress cover so that she could hang it up as soon as she returned home . As she was sealing the box Vicky could see that she was a little watery eyed "Lots of love goes into making these dresses" she whispered .

"I know and lots of hard work" added Vicky "and I really appreciate it . I know I will feel like a million dollars when I wear it ".

The lady gave Vicky a hug . "Be happy , my dear , and have a marvellous wedding and a wonderful life with your lucky young man".

I'm lucky too , thought Vicky , and she was on the verge of tears as they left the shop , but at least they were tears of joy .

When they arrived back at her mum's house Grace suggested that Vicky leave the dress with her until the wedding . Vicky thought that was a good idea and so she took it out of the box and covered it with the dress cover that the little lady had provided , then they hung it up in Vicky's old bedroom . She then thanked her mum for coming with her to buy the most important dress of her life , kissed her and set off home .

Later she rang Liz and told her about the dress and arranged when it would be best to take both Liz and Evie together to get their bridesmaid dresses etc: A Saturday seemed most convenient as Liz worked awkward hours in the week . Evie could come almost any weekend and she often slept over . Evie loved coming to stay with Vicky and Vicky loved having her. Good practise , she thought , for when she had a family of her own , which was looking more likely now . She felt a warm glow pass over her at the thought of having Adam's children .

Soon it was Saturday and Vicky drove to Southampton . She had arranged to meet Adam at the ferry terminal as she knew where that was . Although she only lived about sixty miles from Southampton she didn't often travel there .

She parked near the entrance to the terminal and as the cars were leaving the ferry she saw Adam's BMW in her rear view mirror . Her heart did a flying leap as it always did when she saw him . Suddenly his car stopped and she saw him get out and go around to the passenger door. She couldn't believe her eyes when a stunningly beautiful blonde got out and Adam actually kissed her .The woman waved as she left him beside his car and walked out of the terminal .

Vicky's heart sank and she couldn't believe the surge of jealousy that hit her like a ton of bricks . "Oh , no!" she cried aloud "Please God don't let him have anyone else". She felt faint and panic stricken as her chest tightened and then her mind went into overdrive . Why was he taking her to an hotel and not to his house which was probably just up the road . She knew he wasn't already married or Harry would have told her , but did he have another woman installed there at the moment . The blonde was far more beautiful than she was so what was Adam doing with Vicky anyway . Whatever was she going to do . She could just turn around and drive home…. Then her mobile phone rang and she answered it even though she knew it was Adam .

"Hi , Doughnut , where are you?" he said very cheerfully .

"I'm parked here at the terminal" she answered hoping he didn't notice the trembling in her voice .

"When you see my car follow me to the hotel".

"Okay".

"Are you alright , Sweetheart , you don't sound too good?"

"Just tired" she lied .

"Not too tired , I hope" he laughed "Look let's just get to the hotel and then we can relax". He hung up and a few seconds later he passed her and motioned for her to follow him .

At the hotel they parked and Adam shot straight out of his car and over to hers . As she got out he pulled her into his arms and kissed her passionately but all she could think of was the fact that those same lips had just kissed another woman . As she pulled away he said "Doughnut , you look as if you're going to burst into tears any minute , whatever is the matter?"

"Nothing" she answered trying not to cry .

"You are pleased to be here aren't you?".

"Yes" she murmured quietly "shall we go in?".

Adam knew something was wrong , this was not the Vicky he had spoken to on the phone last night who had been so looking forward to it . What had happened since he had spoken to her then . He had a terrible feeling that Vicky may have changed her mind about marrying him and he felt sick in the pit of his stomach .

They went to reception to check into their room , Adam carried the bags . As soon as they reached the room and he closed the door behind them he dropped the bags onto the floor , looked at Vicky and said quite sternly "Come on out with it , sweetheart , what's all this about?"

She had never heard Adam this serious before . She just burst into tears and blurted out that she had seen him kissing the blonde beauty at the terminal and was worried he didn't love her any more .

"Oh , my poor baby , come here" he said smiling , then holding his hands out he pulled her tightly to his chest " That was Celia , my best friend Toby's fiance . Toby is to be best man at our wedding so you will meet them both soon . I only gave her a lift across from the island because she wanted to do some shopping here and Toby is meeting her later to give her a lift back . Oh , poppet , I can't believe you were so jealous". Secretly he was sighing with relief inside and thanking his lucky stars that that was all that was wrong .

"I'm so very sorry" sobbed Vicky "I can't believe I doubted you but I can't handle ever losing you again".

"You'll never lose me , my darling , I promise you here and now that I will be yours forever as long as you want me" he then kissed her gently "You do believe me , don't you?".

"Of course , sorry I was so silly , please forgive me Darling".

He slowly started to take off her coat and murmured seductively "Shall I show you that I have forgiven you". She smiled up into his handsome face and nodded .

With that he leisurely peeled off the rest of her clothes and began to kiss her all over and as he carried her to the bed she knew she would love him always....the episode about the blonde banished forever....she hoped!

They stayed in bed all day . They were supposed to be dressing and going down for a evening meal but Adam decided to take advantage of the hotel room service and he had their meal brought up to the room along with a large bottle of champagne . Every time he was with Vicky he felt he had something to celebrate and this was no exception . They slept in late on the Sunday morning so they also had breakfast in their room . Luckily the rest of the weekend was perfect .

The next couple of weeks were very busy for Vicky and they just flew by so quickly . There was a big festival at a stately home nearby , which lasted for three days at the end of July each year . Everyone attended in fancy dress and the theme for this year was the Roaring Twenties . It was very lucrative for her but also very hard work . She had to get all the costumes in pristine condition before they went out and then clean them all when they came back . She had finished all the washing , ironing and mending and then realised that there were only two days left in July .

Her birthday was on the 9th of August and she fancied having a barbecue in her garden to celebrate , she thought it might be fun , especially for the her nieces and nephews .She would ask all her family and Liz and Brian so that they could all meet Adam . She decided that the Saturday after her birthday would hopefully be ideal for everyone , and she hoped Adam would be able to stay overnight .

She rang her parents , her brothers and Liz and everyone was delighted to come especially Evie who couldn't wait to talk about the wedding , about being a bridesmaid and wearing a pretty dress and a 'tirara'. "It's a tiara" Vicky had corrected her smiling , but Evie was adamant so 'tirara' it was .

Vicky then rang Diana . She answered "Hello , Diana Moore".

It's Vicky" she said thinking how professional Diana sounded on the phone .

Diana had been James' secretary at his solicitors office and that is where they had met and fell in love . James had wanted Adam to follow in his footsteps and take over the business when he himself retired but Adam had no interest in that line of work . Quickly bringing her thoughts back to the present she heard Diana say "Hello my dear , how are you?"

"I'm fine , is everyone alright at your end" she was mostly referring to Harry .

"Harry has a bit of a tickly cough , but nothing to worry about , I hope" answered Diana sounding a little concerned .

"Oh please do give him my love and tell him I hope he feels better soon".

"I will , he will be so thrilled to know that you've rung . Also having all of the wedding arrangements in full swing he is in his element trying to help and putting a few ideas forward . It is reminding him of his marriage to my mother I think and reminiscing is what Daddy does best at the moment".

"Actually I was ringing to ask if you would all be free on the second Saturday in August , which is the 11th . I've decided to have a barbecue to celebrate my birthday . I've asked my parents , my two brothers and their families and my friend Liz will be there with her husband , Brian . Liz is to be Matron of Honour at the wedding . I would like the most important people in my life to be there so that they can all meet my wonderful new family-to-be".

Diana could sense Vicky was smiling on the other end of the phone ."I'll check with James and Adam and ask him to ring you back later . So long as he is well enough I know wild horses wouldn't stop my father from coming ".

"If coming here and going back on the same day is too much for Harry , I do have two spare bedrooms at my house .You would be welcome to stay here".

"Oh we wouldn't want to impose , my dear , not if Adam is staying with you" she laughed lightly and said "we would be playing gooseberry".

Vicky smiled to herself she hadn't heard that old saying in years .

"Is there a nice hotel or B+B near you?" Diana enquired .

"We do have an excellent pub in the village called the Axe and Compass Inn . It has quite a good reputation for food and accommodation".

"Well as I said I will check with the boys and Adam will let you know as soon as possible . Take care , dear , it was lovely talking to you".

"Bye then , see you soon" said Vicky and she was just about to ring off when Diana asked "Oh Vicky , is Saturday 11th of August your actual birth date".

"No , it's on the 9th but I thought that the weekend would be more convenient for everyone".

"Alright , I'll talk to you soon" and with that Diana rang off .

Then Vicky realised she hadn't even told Adam when her birthday was even though they had discussed their ages that first day on their way back up to the house from the car park . She would have to remember to put her birthday book on the side in the kitchen and then the next time he came she wouldn't forget to ask him .

She reached for a note-pad and began to make out the guest list for her barbecue so that she would know how many to cater for . She also made a list of things she would need to buy like sausages , chicken legs , burgers , onions , rolls and salad . Maybe a cold rice salad would be nice and , of course , she mustn't forget the desserts . She loved cooking and sweets and puddings were her favourites . She may make those herself , still she had a week or so to think about it .

Barbecue day arrived and Liz had offered to come over early to help . Brian dropped her off and said he would be back at 1 pm .

August was a very quiet month for the fancy dress business so Vicky had made sure she had no appointments for today and had advised everyone due to pick up costumes for Saturday or the weekend to call for them on Friday .

She had asked her guests to arrive at 1 o'clock thinking that being lunchtime it would suit most of them .

The sun was shining and she was so thrilled that she had managed to pick such a fine day. She had gone into the garden earlier and placed her large white picnic table with a parasol in the centre on the spacious patio and around it she had arranged the six matching chairs

She also had a wooden picnic table with bench seats that would seat four of her guests , so she placed that on the lawn . She put some pretty bright table clothes on the tables and luckily she also found she had some handy little clips to keep them in place . Her mum had seen some large citrus candles at the garden centre and had mentioned them to her , so she had decided to buy some to place on the tables . When lit they kept all the flies and insects at bay and Vicky thought they were a great idea .

Then she popped a few spare chairs here and there . She didn't think the children would sit down for long .

Adam had asked her to wait until he arrived before she lit the barbecue as he was worried that she would hurt herself . Anyway just as he promised when he had rung to confirm the time , he and his family arrived at 12 noon and after introducing them to Liz , who was busy cutting and buttering rolls , Adam set to work on the barbecue .

Diana asked if there was anything she could do to help , so Vicky asked her to take all the sausages and burgers etc: out of their wrappings and put them on trays ready for Adam to cook on the barbecue . They had decided to cook the chicken legs in the oven in the kitchen earlier to ensure that they were cooked right through . "Then perhaps you could whip the cream for the sweets" Vicky added .

Vicky had got up early that morning and made a Blackberry and Apple pie , a treacle and Walnut tart and a lovely trifle .

"My favourite" Harry had said as he eyed the blackberry and apple pie , then he had taken his coat off in the dining area and gave Vicky a wonderful hug .

"I always bake my own cakes and pastries".

"That's my girl" Harry said looking behind Vicky and smiling at Adam who was just coming in from the garden .

"That's got the barbecue going , now come here a moment" he said pulling her into the hallway . "We haven't said hello properly yet" and he drew her into his arms and kissed her .

When they surfaced she said "I don't think this is a very good idea".

"Why?" said Adam startled .

"Because we have work to do and if you do that again I will whisk you upstairs in a flash". He pulled her towards him again , laughing as he did so , but she quickly slid out of his grip and ran into the kitchen , whispering "Later" as she went .

At 1 o'clock her parents , Grace and Robert , arrived . Then after getting themselves some drinks her father and James went into the garden with Harry . Vicky was thrilled that the men got on so well .

Vicky's brother , Jack , was next to arrive with his wife Sally and the children , Evie and Christopher . Vicky introduced them to Adam , and Sally , taking Vicky to one side , said quietly "He's gorgeous , you lucky thing" Vicky just smiled , silently agreeing whole-heartedly .

Adam shook hands with Evie and Christopher "I'll be your new uncle when Aunty Vicky and I get married" he smiled at them .They seemed very happy about that and skipped off to the garden .

Vicky had put some skittles and garden bowls outside for them to play with , so hopefully that would keep them amused for a while .

Liz's husband , Brian , arrived at the same time as Vicky's other brother David . Brian offered to carry Lisa in for Suzy and Luke toddled along beside his dad .

Suzy was a beauty . She didn't work much because of the twins but now that David had his own photography business she was always on hand to help him . She had a fantastic portfolio of pictures of herself as a model , which David showed to potential clients as an example of his work . He had also created an album of themselves and the twins in case clients wanted family portraits .

As they entered it was Adam's mother who answered the door . "Hello" she smiled "I'm Adam's mother , Diana , and you are?"

"We are Suzy and David and this is Lisa and Luke , the twins".

"Oh Vicky's brother and sister-in-law , so pleased to meet you both". She held out her hand "Vicky's told me so much about you all I feel as if we know each other already".

Immediately Suzy and David knew they were all going to get along famously . Then David turned to Brian and introduced him to Diana .

After all the introductions were made , everyone congregated in the garden .Vicky gave everyone plates and made sure that they all had a drink . "There is fizzy pop , fruit juice or squash for the children , it's in the kitchen on the side near the fridge" . She told them to get their burgers and hot-dogs from Adam and pointed to the dining room table for all the accompaniments . There was a large bowl of salad , another of cold vegetable rice and loads of fried onions for the burgers and hot-dogs . She had also cooked some jacket potatoes because she knew that was Adam's favourite , and after all that they would be enjoying those delicious desserts .

Later whilst they were serving the puddings and desserts Diana asked Vicky for the recipe for the Treacle and Walnut tart . " It's really is delicious , although we will all have to watch our figures if we are still going to fit into our wedding outfits .

Everyone laughed and the men made some comments about women always being on some diet or another . Harry enjoyed his Blackberry and Apple pie and whipped cream . "You make the best pastry I have ever tasted".

"Flattery will get you everywhere Harry" replied Vicky smiling . Harry loved her smile , well he loved Vicky full stop and he was so relieved that she and Adam had found one another .

When everyone had finished eating the girls cleared the tables and filled the dishwasher . At last Vicky was able to sit down and relax for a moment . She sat beside Harry for a while and held his hand . He thanked her for all her hard work and told her how much he had enjoyed it .

"I hope it hasn't tired you out too much . Next time I see you will be on the Bank Holiday weekend at the end of this month . I will be coming over to the island to visit you for a change"

"That will be grand" smiled Harry .

Then much to her surprise her mum came out of the kitchen with a Birthday cake loaded with lighted candles and everybody sang Happy Birthday . Adam held her hand and squeezed it tightly . After she had blown all the candles out , Adam whispered in her ear "Make a wish , did you?".

"It's a secret" she whispered back and he fleetingly kissed the back of her neck .

Suddenly two little children were excitedly jumping up and down demanding that the candles be lit again so that they could take turns to blow them out .

Then it was present opening time . Vicky was quite excited , she loved her birthdays and it was a good excuse for a party . Her parents had bought her some book tokens as she loved to read . Suzy , David and the children gave her a package wrapped in very attractive wrapping paper and when she opened it she discovered a framed portrait of their little family with both parents each holding one of the twins on their lap . Vicky adored it . Attached to the picture was a note which asked Adam and Vicky if they would like David to be the official photographer at their wedding , as a wedding present . Both Adam and Vicky were thrilled .

Diana , James and Harry gave her a very attractive gold bracelet . "It almost matches the necklace you gave to me Harry" she said kissing him and fingering the beautiful locket which she wore around her neck every day . As she thanked Diana and James , Harry smiled and said "It was our pleasure".

Jack and Sally knew that Vicky loved candles so they had bought her a superb set of three holders that looked like wine glasses . They were all different heights and would look great on the mantle piece above the fireplace in the lounge . Vicky still had an open fire and although it was hard to clean she loved it . When it was lit , it gave the room a warm , cosy and romantic atmosphere especially on cold winter nights .

Liz and Brian had bought her some half-round ceramic wall light covers which they knew she had admired when they'd taken her to the apartment that they owned in Carihuela near Torromelinos in Spain the year before . Vicky loved them . Both of them were white but one had lemon flowers which would look lovely in her entrance hall , and she thought she would save the other one with the blue pattern for a wall light fitting she was thinking of putting on the landing at the top of the stairs .

Adam then piped up "I hope you don't mind everyone but I'll give Vicky her present later when we are alone". Everyone laughed and the men made some gaudy comments about it. Her brother Jack then proposed a toast to Vicky and Adam on their engagement last month . They hadn't had a formal celebration because the wedding was now only two months away .

At about 5 pm with little cherubs getting tired everybody started to drift away . Diana , James and Harry set off to the village pub , telling Adam that they would be leaving after lunch the next day .

"Why don't Vicky and I come to the pub for lunch with you , then I can go back with you from there".

"Excellent idea" exclaimed Diana "shall we say 1 pm for lunch . The ferry is at 5 pm so that should work out fine".

Vicky gave them all goodbye hugs and they all thanked her for a super time and Harry said he was looking forward to seeing her the next day .

When everyone had gone and after Vicky had thanked them all so much for the fabulous presents and for their company , she and Adam were alone at last .

Vicky made a pot of tea and they sat together on the sofa with Vicky snuggled up into his shoulder . Adam put his arm around her .

"This is my favourite place in all the world , being here in your arms" she sighed "It's heaven just the two of us".

"When we're married would you mind if there were more that just the two of us".

Vicky looked at him and frowned .

"Well we haven't spoken about children yet . I don't know how you feel about us having a family".

"I'd love to have children , two would be nice , a boy and a girl , if possible in that order".

She wished hard "Besides" she added pointing to the locket "Harry says I have to have a little girl to pass this onto .

Adam squeezed her tightly and kissed the top of her curly hair . "I adore you so much , Doughnut" he murmured huskily as he reached over to his jacket which was on the arm of the sofa . With his free hand he felt into the pocket and drew out an envelope , "Can you possibly get next weekend off". he handed the envelope to her .

As she started to open it she said "If I see all my clients this week by Friday they can take their costumes with them and anyone booked……..Oh! Oh!" she screeched as she began reading the letter and she was ecstatic . This was a voucher for the two of them to enjoy a cream tea and an evening meal , followed by an overnight stay at Thornfield Castle , a medieval hotel , not far from her home .

"Happy Birthday , my Darling".

"Oh Adam , you really shouldn't have , this is far too extravagant".

"Nothing is too good for you , Doughnut" he said flashing another of his amazing smiles and so thrilled knowing that the present he had thought of was more than acceptable. "Besides I'm going to enjoy it with you"

She put her arms around his neck and kissed and kissed and kissed him again.

"You're quite pleased then?". he laughed as he came up for air .

"Pleased! Pleased! It's fabulous and the best present ever!"

They sat back talking about the day and saying how successful it had been and then Adam suggested that she must be really tired after all her hard work and that she definitely deserved to go to bed early .

Vicky smiled knowing exactly what he meant so after the end of such a perfect day she was now going to have a perfect night .

Chapter 9.

THEY awoke quite early the next day and after kissing good morning and both secretly thinking about the fantastic love-making they had enjoyed the previous night , they rose and both showered , dressed and came down for a light breakfast . Neither of them were ravenously hungry , not for food anyway , and of course they had a large lunch to look forward to at the pub .

Vicky tidied up , although there wasn't too much to do because the men had cleared up the garden after tea yesterday and the women had helped to clean the kitchen . So they just ate toast and drank coffee . "Would you like some homemade marmalade on your toast?"

"Goodness me , Doughnut , you are a woman of many talents , homemade marmalade! I'll be in for a treat when I'm married to you" the smile of satisfaction on his face was priceless .

"I didn't say that I made it" she laughed " I bought it at the village fete . Old Florrie who lives down at Bradley

Road makes it and everyone in the village who buys it laughs and says its aphrodisiac .

"Do you really think I need it then?" he said with a twinkle in his eye . He crossed the kitchen , winked at her , then drew her to him and looked deeply into her gorgeous eyes .

"I don't think I had better answer that as I may incriminate myself." she returned the look and added "shall we sit here and eat our breakfast or take it into the garden?".

"Let's go outside , it's a cracking day".

They both carried the trays out , then Vicky brought Snowy's cage out with them . The little budgie was chirping at all the other birds in the garden .

"I love all birds" she then pointed out some green finches on the feeder that was filled with sunflower seeds . Whilst they sat enjoying their breakfast they also saw sparrows , starlings , robins , blue tits and even a little wren . Her garden was a wonderful haven for many birds . In one corner there was a large sycamore tree and against the wood fencing there were many shrubs , bushes and conifers . On the wall at the back of the house she had placed three nesting boxes and most years blue tits or great tits would nest there . She told Adam it was always a thrill to watch the baby birds learning how to fly . Behind the potting shed at the top of the garden she had made a little path with small stones so that at night the hedgehogs could walk around the shed to the lawn at the side . Every night they came through a hole that she had made in the fence behind the big tree and as they were carnivorous she always put cat food out for them . She said she must be the only person who bought cat food at the supermarket who didn't have a cat .

As Vicky was telling Adam all of this he felt so full of love for this very beautiful , kind , caring , adorable lady.

By now they had finished their breakfast so they cleared away and put Snowy back into the lounge . Vicky suddenly realised that Adam was leaving the pub with his parents and Harry immediately after the meal to go back to the island . So now would be their only time alone together until next weekend .

She offered to help him pack his overnight bag , so off they went to the bedroom . Of course the bag didn't get packed for another hour but they both enjoyed their goodbye gestures . They got up and showered again and got themselves ready to go out to lunch . They were taking Vicky's car because James had driven Adam's to the pub the night before .

Arriving at the restaurant of the pub where they had arranged to meet , Vicky waved to Harry and Diana who were already sat at the table . James had gone to get the menu and order some drinks . He called Adam over to help him whilst Vicky sat down . Diana said the accommodation was superb and that they had managed to find a downstairs bedroom for Harry . Of course at home they had had the stair-lift fitted for Harry which he was very grateful for as he found it difficult to walk too far unaided .

Lunch was very pleasant and everyone commented on the delicious food but all too soon it was time to say goodbye again . Vicky hugged Diana and James and they thanked her for a lovely weekend . She hugged and kissed

Harry and he said he was looking forward to her visit on the August Bank Holiday weekend .

"What's this then , Grandfather , making secret dates with my young lady are you?" Adam made everyone laugh .

"It's just that you have been so kind to come and visit me here , I thought I might come to visit you all at the end of the month if that's okay?"

"That's fantastic . We could stay at my apartment in Cowes and then go to the house from there . I actually remember something about a re-union at the yacht club that weekend as well , I'll check it out . But don't forget your birthday treat this coming weekend" .

"How could I forget that" she said with a gleam in her eye.

By this time Diana , James and Harry were all settled in the car waiting . So Adam gave her tender kiss and promised to ring her as soon as they reached home .

She waved as they disappeared from sight , got into her little red car and drove home feeling quite melancholy after such a fun filled weekend .

The trip to the castle the next weekend was out of this world . They were welcomed at the hotel by a valet who parked the car for them . Inside they were escorted to the library , where the head waiter in his smart livery had their cream tea brought to them . Delicious little pastries , cakes , brownies and scones were delicately served on a three tiered cake stand . The china teapot with matching milk and sugar bowl were all brought to the table as were the jam and cream for the scones . They sat in winged chairs and were told that King Henry VIII and Anne

Boleyn had stayed there in approximately 1534 and they had sat in this very room . The head waiter , Jaime , who was Spanish and had been at the hotel for many years , came back to ask if everything was to their satisfaction . Vicky , who had learnt Spanish at school and still spoke it if she went to Spain , conversed easily with him and he was very impressed that she had taken the trouble to talk to him in his native tongue . Adam was also impressed .

After the delicious tea they went to their room to unpack and then decided to go for a leisurely walk in the garden . Then before they knew it , it was time to shower and change for dinner . Although their room was called the Camelot Suite it was decorated more like a Tudor room . There was a four-poster bed with tapestry designed drapes and matching upholstery on the chairs . There was a writing desk cum dressing table , two beautiful wardrobes plus an en-suite bathroom . The walls were panelled in what looked like rosewood and Vicky felt as if she had been transported back in time .

"You're quiet , Doughnut".

"I am just totally knocked out by all of this opulence , I have never stayed anywhere as special as this before , and I was only twenty seven , it wasn't even a special birth date".

"Well , you are very special to me and as far as I'm concerned you deserve the best of everything" he walked around the bottom of the bed and held out his arms.

"You are so kind" she just fell into his embrace and they revelled in each others kisses . After a while Adam spoke "Let's get ready for dinner and afterwards we can have an early night . We may as well use the bed as much as possible , it cost enough". he smiled as he said it . He was only joking . He paid himself a reasonably good salary from his business and he hadn't spent a lot of money over the last couple of years . He could well afford this and more and he so enjoyed treating Vicky .

Vicky had brought a strapless black lace dress with a matching bolero top to wear this evening . She asked Adam to help her with the zip . She would normally have worn an ornate necklace with this outfit , but no , tonight she wore the locket that Harry had given to her . She did however bring the lovely gold bracelet that Adam's parents and Harry had given to her on her birthday last week and , of course , she wore her beautiful ruby engagement ring . She stooped to put on her black sling-back shoes and thought how much better her ankle was now .

Adam dressed in his dinner suit , a white dress shirt and black bow tie . She thought he looked splendid .

They looked the perfect couple as Jaime ushered them to a secluded table in the corner , where candles and flowers adorned the centre . The setting was intimately romantic and Vicky felt as if they were in heaven .

They enjoyed oak-smoked salmon and shrimp cocktail to start , followed by beef in port wine with fresh vegetables . Then there was the dessert , the course that Vicky loved the most . It was a chocolate truffle torte with a mouth-watering sauce . To follow that there was a selection of English and continental cheeses with an assortment of crackers . Adam had red wine with the meal but as she wasn't a fan of that she had a small glass of Rose`. They finished their meal with Gaelic coffee .

"Have you had enough to eat , Sweetheart?".

"Too much really , but it was all delicious thank you" she let out a huge sigh "perhaps we should try to work some of this off" she indicated the dance floor . Through an archway to their left was a small dance floor and a string quartet were playing romantic love songs.

I can think of a much better way to work a meal off than dancing , he smiled to himself knowing that it was most likely they would be getting some extremely strenuous exercise later that night anyway .

As they danced she felt a shiver of pleasure running through her whole body and he held her so close she thought they were almost one entity . After several dances they decided to wander outside for a breath of fresh air before retiring to their magnificent bedroom .

Outside in the grounds it was almost as magical as inside and Vicky's imagination ran wild as she pictured what may have occurred here all those years ago .

Adam was worried she may get cold but she came up with the old cliché that she had his love to keep her warm . They returned to the hotel and said goodnight to Jaime and then climbed the spiral staircase to their room . Adam closed and locked the door behind them then took Vicky in his arms and whilst looking almost provocatively into each others eyes they slowly undressed one another and contemplated another night fulfilling all of their sexual fantasies .

On the Sunday they enjoyed a delicious breakfast in the hotel and said their goodbyes and a special thank you to Jaime . At the reception desk as he paid the bill Adam noticed a set of chocolate bars in a commemorative pack . It was Henry VIII and his six wives so he bought a pack for Vicky as a momento .

I don't really need anything to remind me of this , she thought , as she took the lovely gift from him , I shall never ever forget it in my whole life . She then thanked him with a kiss. They drove back to her house and as Adam had a lot of business to deal with this coming week he would go back to Southampton straight after lunch . He was staying at his house there for the next week and then they would be staying at his apartment on the island over the bank holiday which they suddenly realised was the next weekend . The bank holiday fell on the 27th this year . When it was time for him to leave they kissed at the front door and , as always , he promised to ring as soon as he got home .

Vicky sat in her lounge after he had left and could not believe how hectic her social life had become since meeting Adam .

Was it really only three months ago that she had strolled into Harry's garden at the magical house and this exciting adventure had begun . How quickly one's life could change , she thought , but for her at least , it had been for the better .

Her little bird flew from his cage onto her head . She lifted him down onto her hand and he was chirping away . "Oh , Snowy" she said "how lucky I am to have found Adam".

She then thought she should be un-packing her weekend case and preparing herself for the week ahead . She was not too busy with clients this week but there was always plenty of sewing , ironing and mending to catch up on .

She went to bed early that night and fell asleep hugging one of her pillows as she felt rather cold and alone in the bed by herself . She thought about the wedding in October and hoped it would come around soon as she was so looking forward to the time when she would never have to go to bed on her own again .

Chapter 10.

THIS Bank Holiday weekend Vicky was going to meet the beautiful blonde , Celia and her fiance Toby , who was going to be Best man at their wedding . She was very nervous, almost to the point of nausea , because she had not met any of Adam's friends before .

Adam had rung her midweek to suggest that if she could possibly get away on Friday evening and drive down to him , then they could stay at the house in Southampton that night and get the ferry to the island the next day .They would be staying at his apartment in Cowes over the weekend and from there they could go to the yacht club to meet his friends on Saturday evening . Then on Sunday they were invited to lunch and tea at his parents and Vicky could not wait to see Harry again .

She had arranged for everyone to pick up the fancy dress they had pre-booked for the weekend by Thursday evening and all of her appointments on Friday were all booked before lunch time. She had packed a weekend case , although she was not quite sure what to pack for the Saturday evening . Oh , drat , she said to herself , they will just have to take me as they find me . So she plucked the ever faithful little black dress from the wardrobe and popped it into her case .

Friday soon came around . She dropped Snowy off at Jack and Sally's at teatime . Evie and Christopher always loved it when Vicky came around especially as she always took along a large bag of their favourite sweets as a reward for being good and looking after the little bird for her .

She told them she would be returning on the ferry early on Tuesday morning and that she would let them know as soon as she got home .

She was all ready so she set off in her little car . Adam had sent her an e-mail , earlier in the week , with a map to his house so she felt quite confident of arriving safely , and of course she had her mobile phone to ring him if she got lost .

Because it was Friday evening the traffic around Salisbury was horrendous , so she was held up there for quite a while .

She eventually got to Adam's , which to her amazement she found straight away , and she parked her car in the space he had marked on the map . She sat in her car and as it was beginning to get dark she decided to ring him .

He answered immediately "Adam Moore" he purred in his usual husky voice .

"It's me" she sounded petrified .

"Are you alright , Doughnut , not lost are you?" He sounded very concerned .

"No , I think I'm outside your house but could you please come and get me?".

"Of course , Darling , just hang on a moment". He turned off the phone and went straight to the front door , he immediately switched on the outside light , which he should have done earlier , and he saw Vicky's car in his parking space outside .

He went to the car and as soon as she saw him she opened the car door and got out and flung herself into his arms and started crying . He held her closely "What is it ,Sweetheart

has someone frightened you?". She shook her head but still carried on crying . Still holding onto her he removed her case from the boot , locked the car and took her inside .

He locked the door behind them and he led her through to the lounge then sat her gently on the sofa and asked her if she would like a drink .

"Just tea , please" she managed to whisper .

She was still wondering what had upset her , then she thought it might have been the relief of seeing Adam again , because she had missed him terribly .

She glanced around the room whilst he was gone and thought how homely it looked . She was quite surprised considering Adam's age and the fact that he was a single man living on his own . There was a cream coloured soft leather suite with large colourful cushions situated almost in the centre of the room , and there was a mahogany coffee table and matching hi-fi units . The luxurious carpet was very plush , and in front of the flame effect fire , a cream fur rug that looked so inviting . Suddenly she wanted to be stretched out on that rug with Adam kissing and caressing her naked body and taking her to the indescribable heights she had come to expect from their lovemaking . She was still daydreaming about it when he returned from the kitchen .

Adam had got them both tea , he placed it on the coffee table and then sat beside her on the sofa . He put his arm around her and handed the tea to her . She was holding the mug tightly with both hands yet she was still shaking like a leaf.

"Whatever is the matter?".

"I don't know" she whispered "I'm sure I will be alright in a minute".

"Can I do anything to help?" He said anxiously.

"No , please don't worry , this will help" she indicated the tea .

"I can't help worrying about you , Darling , I love you".

"and I love you too . Thank you for being so concerned . Maybe I was just so relieved that I had arrived okay . The journey was rather fraught with all the weekend traffic . Maybe I was nervous about finding your house , although the map you sent was fantastic , I found it straight away".

"Well you're here now , Poppet , safe and sound with me" he murmured softly .

After they'd finished the tea she felt a little calmer .

She leaned into him and he put his hand under her chin and tilted her mouth up towards his . Something always happened to her when he kissed her and even she was not sure what it was . All she knew was that all the worry , uneasiness and tension that had built up inside of her was melting away as his kiss deepened and all she could think about was him and his bewitchingly tender touch and the intense love she felt for him .The kiss seemed everlasting but when it eventually finished she felt quite calm inside and much better.

Why did that happen to me? she puzzled , it never had before .Why did she feel so insecure ?

As she was thinking Adam spoke "Why don't we turn in now , you will feel much better after a good night's sleep" he suggested .

Vicky just laughed "I actually did not have sleep in mind".

"That's my girl" he said giving her a playful squeeze . "I will show you around the house in the morning".

"He took the cups back to the kitchen then carried her case up to his bedroom . He had an en-suite bathroom so Vicky went to clean her teeth and freshen her face before returning to the bedroom .

Adam used the bathroom while she sorted the clothes from her case . She looked around the sizeable bedroom , he had a king-size bed and the furnishings were all black and white with black silk sheets on the bed . Very masculine , but she loved it .

By the time Adam returned to the bedroom , naked , Vicky was in bed . She watched intently as he walked towards the bed . She took in his every muscle and sinew of his tremendous body and she couldn't take her eyes off of his magnificent manhood . Her thoughts were wandering to what that body did to her when he said "Move over doughnut , that's my side" he was smiling that infectious smile of his .

Vicky moved to the middle of the bed as he slid between the sheets and lay beside her . He then enveloped her in his arms and all her anxieties , if she had any, just dissolved into nothingness .

She turned in his arms and looked affectionately into his soft , warm brown eyes and as they began to make love she thought , we're together now and we're going to be together forever , I'm sure.

Next morning Vicky woke up to Adam bringing her tea in bed .He was already dressed . "Oh , you are spoiling me" she said "What time is it?".

"9-30".

"Goodness I'm not used to laying in this late . What are we going to do today?"

"After I have shown you around the house , we can go to town if you like".

"That will be nice , I have never shopped in Southampton before".

"I need to call into my office for a moment to see if there are any urgent messages , you don't mind , do you?"

"Not at all!".

Vicky drank her tea and then asked Adam if she could use the shower .

"Of course , I'll show you where to find everything you need".

She had soon showered and washed her hair then she dressed in knee-length trousers and an attractive short sleeved top .She went downstairs and walked into the kitchen , she had remembered where that was from last night when Adam had fetched her a drink .

He smiled broadly as she entered and came over to plant another juicy kiss on her welcoming lips "Tea and toast , or would you like something else?".

" Toast will be fine , thank you , it's a little late for anything more" she paused for a second then added "could I please have coffee instead of tea".

"No problem" he fetched the bread from the bread container and popped it into the toaster then put the coffee on , " and while that's doing I'll show you around the house , then you will know where everything is .After all you will be living here soon". He sounded so thrilled when he said that .

The house was on three floors so they started at the top . On this floor there were two large bedrooms and a bathroom , all very tastefully decorated and furnished beautifully . On the next floor down was Adam's large bedroom with the en-suite bathroom , which she was already familiar with , a walk-in wardrobe and another bedroom that Adam used as a study . Then on the ground floor was the exquisite lounge , a charming dining room , complete with a large mahogany table and six carvers similar to his parents dining set . Perhaps they had the same taste in furniture? .There was also an elaborate bar in one corner . The kitchen had state of the arts units and all the mod cons any woman could ever wish for .There was also a separate loo in the cloakroom near the front door . Outside the front door there were steps going down to the road so Vicky asked Adam if there was anything underneath the house .

"The garage and storage space is beneath the house but the vehicle access to that is at the rear of the building so my car is there at the moment". He pointed to a door on the same wall as the kitchen door and told her that this was the access to the stairs leading down to the garage .

"It's a lovely house and so tastefully decorated" she commented as they walked back into the kitchen .

"I have only had it for about a year , as you know I spend quite a lot of time on the island".

"Sailing?"

"Yes , and visiting my family , at least once a week".

They sat at the breakfast bar and ate their toast , Adam had tea and he poured Vicky the coffee she had asked for . When they had finished they put the crockery and cutlery into the dishwasher and were ready to leave .

"I will have to get my coat from my car". Vicky had forgotten to bring it in the night before.

"We shall go together , then we can walk around the side of the house and down the steps to the garage" .

After Vicky had fetched her coat they walked down the steps at the side of the house and he held her hand and that made her feel a little more secure .

They eventually reached the town and parked near Adam's office . They arrived at the office and he tapped in the security code to unlock the door . Today was Saturday and the office was officially closed so he needed to turn off the alarms .

Vicky sat in his office whilst he checked to see if his secretary had left any messages . He got all the information he wanted from the telephone answer machine and the fax so they locked up and left .

They decided to have lunch at a lovely Italian restaurant that Adam often frequented . Vicky had lasagne and salad and Adam decided to have his favourite Italian dish , Spaghetti Bolognese . They also had some very delicious Italian ice-cream and coffee afterwards . When they had finished she thanked him with a kiss . He then settled the bill and as they left he held his hand out to her and she clasped it tightly .

He told her he wanted to buy her a new outfit but , of course , she would not hear of it . "You have already spent too much on me these last few weeks".

"I insist" he said and he held her hand firmly as they crossed the busy road to an exquisite boutique . How would Adam know about this place , she thought , he must have brought all his ex-girlfriends here . Those little green monsters were dancing up and down in front of Vicky's eyes . Stop it Vicky , she said to herself , you're getting jealous again . "This is so nice , how did you know about it ?" she enquired innocently .

"Mother uses this place quite regularly and recommends it to all of her friends".

Oh dear , Vicky felt terrible , how could she ever doubt him after all they had done and said to each other since they had met .

Although she protested Adam bought her a new outfit . A stunning emerald green dress with a splattering of sequins and a matching bag and shoes . Vicky felt as if she was on a catwalk when she emerged from the changing room in the boutique .

Adam's face was a picture . "You look absolutely stunning , Doughnut" he said , his eyes almost popping out of his head . He had never seen her looking so lovely . The dress fitted perfectly around her elegant curves and he knew he was going to be the proudest man at the yacht club that night with Vicky on his arm .

She got changed and handed the items to the assistant who folded the dress carefully and put all the purchases in bags . Adam paid and as they left the shop he whispered in her ear. "You looked amazing in that and I can't wait to take you out and show you off tonight" She accepted the compliment and thanked him once again .

"It was my pleasure , my beautiful Doughnut" he smiled and squeezed her hand .

"Do you know if there is are any hairdressers nearby . I would like to get my hair done but it is rather short notice?"

"I'm sure we can find one somewhere". Adam scanned a few shops and saw that there was a hairdressers just across the road . "Let's go and check . Perhaps you could have it put up like you did on the night of your friend's retirement party , it looked fabulous then".

They entered the shop and sure enough they could fit her in immediately .

She was feeling much better now and neither she nor Adam mentioned the crying fit from the night before . Adam went off and left Vicky in the salon saying he would be back in half an hour . Although the stylist said it would take a little longer he wanted to be back to pay for it .He had so enjoyed treating Vicky , he had not done this for a long time and he just wanted to take care of her forever .

Later in the afternoon as they were getting ready to go out Vicky felt really funny in her stomach . She didn't know if it was excitement or fear . She knew she would be meeting the blonde bombshell , who looked like a high class model or an actress . She knew Adam was going to be proud to introduce her to everyone but would she let him down , she hoped not .

Adam called to ask if she had finished in the bathroom.

"Almost" she called back . Come on Vicky stop feeling nervous and get on with it , she said to herself as she put the finishing touches to her lipstick . All done , she emerged from the bathroom in just her underwear and stockings .Adam looked so lovingly yet lustfully at her ."You are so gorgeous" he told her .

"Just go on and use the bathroom or we will be late" she scolded him , but smiled as she said it , knowing that if he did not they would be on the bed naked in no time at all .

By the time Adam had finished in the bathroom Vicky was ready except for the zip at the back of her dress . "Could you zip me up , please?" she asked .

"I will enjoy un-zipping you a lot more later". He pulled the zip up and she walked away from him to the dressing table to pick up Harry's locket .

"Turn around , sweetheart" he sounded so sexy. She did so ."You look absolutely stunning".

"Thank you" she almost felt herself blush

"I love you so much , my Darling , and I shall be the proudest man there tonight".

"Oh Adam you say the sweetest things".

He wanted to kiss her senseless but she had only just finished her make-up and he did not want to spoil it .

He finished dressing and very soon they were on their way out . He looked so handsome Vicky thought as he locked the door and held her arm as they went down the steps to the car , which he had left at the front of the house . He had put their overnight bags into the boot earlier as they were going to the island on the ferry , then straight to the yacht club and on to the flat afterwards .

As he opened the car door for her , she seemed to falter a little .

"Is your ankle still hurting , are the new shoes too high for you , are you sure you're alright?" he was fussing over her , but secretly she wallowed in it .

She settled herself into the car and looked lovingly up into his eyes and smiled . "I'm perfectly alright , but thank you for caring so much".

He leant down , put his head in the car and kissed her so fleetingly that her heart fluttered.

They arrived at the dock fairly quickly and were ushered onto the ferry . The journey would take approximately an hour so they went upstairs to the bar and Adam ordered drinks .

They were sat at a table chatting when a rather large man approached them . Vicky looked up as he said "Adam , old chap, it's great to see you".

Adam stood and greeted him with a handshake . "Hello Eric".

"Going to the reunion at the yacht club are you" he was still holding onto Adam's hand . "Haven't seen you for ages . Are you going to introduce me to this gorgeous young lady here?"

"Oh sorry , Eric ,this is Vicky , my fiance" .

Vicky realised that that was the first time she had heard Adam say the word fiance and it sounded wonderful and he had put the emphasis on 'my fiance' as if trying to get a point over to him .

"Vicky , this is an old friend , Eric".

Eric put his hand out to shake Vicky's and as she took it she felt a little uneasy . "Pleased to meet you", she said with trepidation . Goodness , she thought , I hope all Adam's friends are not like this one .

They sat together for the rest of the journey , Adam and Eric reminiscing about old times . Eric was alone , he had not brought a partner . Apparently he had been married and divorced twice , Vicky was not surprised .

When the time came to go back to their cars , Eric bid them farewell and said he would see them later . In the car Vicky said nothing to Adam of her misgivings .

They arrived at the club and Adam got out of the car and went around to open the door for her . He helped her out and held her very tightly and said "I think this is going to be a night to remember"

Little did he know how prophetic his words would be .

Chapter 11.

THEY left their coats in the cloakroom and walked into the large function room . Adam sat Vicky at a corner table and went to the bar to order some drinks .

Suddenly she looked up and saw him talking to a handsome couple , then she realised it was the blonde bombshell with her normally long straight hair styled in the exact same way as her own , up on top with little strands of hair curling in front of her ears .

Oh drat! Thought Vicky , I wish I had kept mine down , but too late to worry about that now.

They were coming towards her and she was dreading it .

"Sweetheart , this is Celia and Toby".

Vicky raised her hand to shake hands with Celia "Pleased to meet you" she lied .

"Ditto" said the blonde and her hand felt limper than a leaf of dead lettuce .

"Toby" Adam said , indicating his friend.

Toby shook her hand firmly "So pleased to meet you at last" and as he stooped to kiss her on her cheek , he whispered in her ear , "Adam has told me so much about you and yes he was right you are adorable". His smile was infectious .

She returned the smile and said "I'm so pleased to meet you too". She really liked Toby and wondered whatever he was doing wasting his time with that Celia woman . Celia sat down beside her and her perfume was so over-powering ….Vicky felt sick.

They all talked in general about the boats and their occupations . Vicky decided to sit quietly and listen but say nothing .

The music started and Toby and Celia and several other couples went onto the dance floor

"Would you like to dance , Doughnut?"

"Not yet , maybe later", she looked quite sad .

"Are you alright ? you seem a little subdued". he guessed that Vicky was not very pleased about the events of the last ten minutes

"I only feel a little strange because I don't really know anyone as well as you do , so we have nothing in common to talk about".

"You know me and that's all that matters isn't it?" he said with a smile .

"Yes, of course" Vicky returned the smile and he bent to kiss her lightly on the lips .

"I'll just get some more drinks" he picked up their glasses "same again?"

"Yes please" she answered . She was just sticking to fruit juice and lemonade tonight .

The minute Adam left her alone the creep Eric came and sat down beside her and put his hand on her knee . She was horrified and tried to move away .

"Hello again , Gorgeous" he leered at her. He had obviously already had too much to

drink , what with the bar on the ferry and now here.

"Please remove your hand" Vicky said curtly .

"Oh don't get all prissy darling", he leaned towards her , his foul breath too close for comfort .

She stood up and moved out onto the dance floor just as Adam was returning with the drinks . "I would love to dance now , if you still want to?".

"Certainly , Sweetheart". He put the drinks down on the table , nodded to Eric and swept Vicky into his arms.

She did not mention anything about Eric but decided to hold Adam close and enjoy the dance and try to forget that that little episode had ever happened .

Just as the compere announced that the buffet was being served in the lounge bar , Vicky decided to go to the ladies room. Celia followed her .

They had both used the loo and were washing their hands when Celia said something that totally shocked Vicky .

"This wedding of yours will never happen , you know".

"I beg your pardon?"

"This farce between you and Adam".

Vicky was astounded ."Whatever do you mean!".

"He loves me , that's why".

By now Vicky was totally shocked .

"I know how it feels when he walks naked from the shower and slides between those silky black sheets , then takes you to heights you could have only ever dreamed of before".

Vicky wanted to cry , she picked up her bag and ran out of the ladies room . Where would she go , her heart was thumping , her chest felt so tight she could hardly breath . Adam caught sight of her . "Sweetheart , I've brought you some food"

She was panicking , she could not make a scene here in front of all of his friends so she followed him back to their table .

He put the food down in front of her but she just could not face it . "I'm not really hungry"her voice quivered .

"But you must be , we haven't eaten since this afternoon". Adam looked extremely confused .

"I'm okay , thank you".

Toby had arrived at the table with the food he had brought back for himself and that woman . He called out to her and she had the gall to swan back across the dance floor like a model on a catwalk and sit down as if nothing had been said .

Vicky was stunned into silence . After the others had eaten and the plates had been collected she excused herself and went back to the ladies room . She went in and was physically sick . She felt dreadful . What was she going to do , how could she even face Adam after this . She patted her face with a tissue and looked in the mirror. She thought she looked awful . After a few more moments she composed herself and returned to the dance floor .

She looked across at the table and it was empty , where had they all gone . She looked around and could not see Adam anywhere , she thought that a breath of fresh air might do her good so she walked outside . She turned left to walk along the terrace and heard voices coming from around the end of the building . She turned the corner and her heart clenched in horror as she witnessed Adam and Celia in a clinch , kissing passionately .

She turned around and ran back inside , at the same time fumbling in her evening bag for the cloakroom ticket . She found it and went to ask the assistant for her coat .

Then she went outside and started running although she did not know where . She passed some couples in the car park so she slowed down a little . Her ankle was still painful at times especially when she wore high heels .

Meanwhile Adam was frantically searching for her inside . When he went to the cloakroom the lady said she had gone so he ran outside . He saw a couple walking back towards the club and asked if they'd seen a young lady walking this way .

"Yes , she went left at the gate" the gentleman replied.

Adam thought he may as well take the car and he quickly drove off in that direction . It was very dark now but he suddenly saw a twinkle of green sequins in the lights of his car . He slowed down and opened the passenger window "Vicky" he called . She ignored him and walked on . She had no idea where she was going , the pins were falling from her hair and the night breeze was blowing it around her eyes and it was sticking to her face . She was crying so profusely she could hardly see , and the tears were dripping off her chin . The last thing she wanted to do at this moment was talk to him .

He drove a little ahead of her and stopped the car . He got out and walked back towards her . She tried to turn around and walk back the way she had come but he caught up with her ."Vicky , whatever is the matter?" he asked as he caught hold of her arm .

"How can you ask me that after what I just saw" she shouted , pushing him away .

"What?"

"You kissing her!".

"I did not kiss her!".

"You did , I saw it with my own eyes" she shouted again and the tears still kept coming .

Adam had never seen Vicky cross before . "Please Vicky let's go home and talk about this".

"I can't go home" she cried "there are no more ferries tonight".

"I mean my apartment , let's go back there"

"No!" she screamed .

"Look you can't stay out here all night , just let me take you back there even if you don't want to talk to me" he pleaded with her as he placed his hand in the small of her back to lead her back to the car.

"Don't touch me" she snapped , she was still crying .

They reached the car and got in . He drove the few minutes it took to get to his apartment and Vicky did not wait for Adam to come around to help her out , she just got out and stomped up the path . Adam almost forgot their overnight bags and went to fetch them from the boot . Vicky came back and snatched her bag from him and then followed him to the door . He keyed in a code to open the door and they went to the lift in silence and rode to the third floor . The lift door opened and he stood back to let her go first then took the key from his pocket to open the door.

"Would you like a drink?".

"No thank you" she snapped again .

"Vicky , please don't be like this". he spoke softly.

She just howled louder . Then she asked "Which is your bedroom?". He pointed towards a door . "Well I won't be in it tonight" she yelled walking to the room next door , she opened it , went in and flung her bag on the bed . She then sat on it with her head in her hands sobbing copiously .

A few minutes later Adam brought her a cup of tea . "Have this , Doughnut , it might help".

"Don't you Doughnut me" she screeched .

Adam was beside himself with grief . "Please Vicky talk to me".

"I don't want to , you lied to me".

"When?"

"All the time" she sniffed .

"I did not"

"Then why were you kissing her?".

"I was not".

"You were!".

"Vicky , look at me".

"No!".

"Vicky , please look at me".

"No!"

"Right , I am going to stay here all night if I have to, until you look me in the eye".

She looked at him .

"Now will you please listen to me" he said softly " I was not kissing her , she was kissing me".

"It definitely did not look like that to me".

"Well it's true . After you went to the ladies room she got me to go outside with her and then she sprung it on me , telling me that she did not love Toby and never had . She told me that she had loved me ever since she had first met me and had only gone out with Toby because she knew that as we were best friends she would at least get to see me sometimes . Apparently she thought she could win me over in time but I was never interested in her at all , not ever . I was telling her that there was no chance of anything ever happening between us as I was totally and completely in love with you and then she pounced"

"But I saw she had her arms around your neck , kissing you full on the mouth and you were holding her wrists .You certainly looked as if you were enjoying it to me".

"I was trying to pry her hands off of my neck but she had a grip like a boa constrictor".

"She's a vicious snake anyway" spat Vicky .

"Darling , please believe me" Adam pleaded . He leaned forward to kiss her when she suddenly remembered what Celia had told her in the ladies room .

She pulled further away from him ,"Get away from me , don't you dare touch me , I hate you!" she screame, tears still streaming down her cheeks .

Adam was so taken aback he looked her straight in the eyes . "You don't really mean that do you ?" he said sadly .

Oh God ! why had she ever said that , she knew she still loved him intensely .

He repeated "You didn't mean it , did you?" he sounded as if his heart was about to break. .

She shook her head "I'm sorry , I feel so hurt maybe I just wanted to hurt you too".

"I'm already hurting" there was a faint trace of bitterness in his voice .

"Well it's your own fault , now leave me alone , maybe we can talk in the morning".

Adam rose from the bed and walked dejectedly out of the room and closed the door behind him.

Vicky tried to compose herself , she knew she would not be able to sleep but she may as well try . Oh drat! she remembered she could not reach the zip at the back of the dress . She would either have to sleep in it or ask Adam to unzip her .

She got up from the bed and quietly opened the door and walked towards his bedroom door . She balled her hand into a fist and as she raised it to knock the door her arm halted in mid air , then her heart broke in two as she heard Adam quietly sobbing on the other side of the door .

She was beside herself with sadness .How had all this happened , from being blissfully happy a couple of hours ago to both of them feeling so wretched now . She gently tapped the door .

"Just a minute" she heard him say . After a little while he called "Come in".

He was sat on the edge of the bed and as she walked towards him he stood up .

"I can't undo the zip" she murmured . She turned around and after he had unzipped the dress he held her arm .

"I do not want you to touch me"

"Vicky , PLEASE" his eyes were pleading with her .

"She touched you and you still smell of that disgusting perfume she was wearing .Why don't you have a shower" She began to walk away .

"Vicky , please stay ". He sounded so pitiful , so she turned around and followed him as he walked into the en-suite bathroom . The dress was still on her shoulders but was unzipped .

He undressed and opened the shower cubicle and turned on the shower . She stared at him in awe and couldn't tear her eyes away as she watched him soaping himself all over . Oh how she loved every part of this wonderful man , his tousled hair , his gorgeous face , his beautifully toned body , his soft warm heart , his very soul , his everything . At that precise moment her whole body ached for him

After he had showered , and even though the water was still running , he opened the door and put one hand out to her but she did not move . He then held both hands out "Please come" she could see the pain in his eyes and could not resist him . She let the dress drop to the floor , stepped out of it , and still in her lacy underwear she walked towards him and took his hands . He pulled her into the shower and closed the door , enfolding her in his arms he kissed her more thoroughly and deeply than he ever had before .

"I have never done this before" she said , drawing away from the kiss but still looking deeply into his eyes .

"Done what?".

"Made love in a shower".

"Neither have I" he replied huskily.

And as the water cascaded over them Vicky wished with all her heart that it would wash all the terrible hurt away .

Vicky woke first next morning . She looked at Adam laying asleep beside her . Had she had a terrible nightmare…no… she remembered the shower .

When they had made love there she had never before climaxed so fiercely , so fully , nor so incredibly in all her life . The emotion was so high , the deep love between them so evident .

Please God , she thought , let me try to forget what happened yesterday , but she could not. She looked at Adam again , she loved him so much her heart ached and she knew she would die for him if she had to .

Just then he stirred so she closed her eyes and pretended to be asleep . He awoke and propped himself up on one elbow and looking lovingly at her he whispered " My own darling Vicky , I adore you so very much , please God let her believe that I want only her forever more".

She pretended to stir and he kissed her gently on the lips and she opened her eyes and smiled . Then their mouths met fleetingly again and he nipped and pecked and softly sucked on her lips , she reciprocated and the sensation for them both was indescribable.

He ended the kiss and looked into her eyes with immeasurable passion "Do you forgive me my Darling?"

"For what?"

"For hurting you last night even though I never meant to and it really was not my fault".

"Before I answer that , I need to tell you something". She proceeded to tell him about the episode in the ladies room when Celia had mentioned the love-making and the black silk sheets .

Adam was horrified . " It's no wonder you were furious with me . I swear to you now , on my grandfather's life" and Vicky knew he would never do that lightly , "that I have never slept with or even wanted to sleep with that conniving , vindictive bitch . The only thing I feel for her is pity" then he added "The only explanation I can come up with is that I had a house-warming party a few months before I met you and she must have sneaked into my bedroom , seen the black sheets and the en-suite and imagined the rest . You do believe me don't you , Vicky" the emotion in his voice was palpable.

"I do believe you and forgive you .Will you please forgive me for believing what she said, when I should have known that you would never do anything to hurt me , ever".

He drew her gently into his arms and once again kissed her so intimately. He looked at her again "I thought this weekend was going to be like a dream but instead it turned into a nightmare , thanks to that wicked woman".

"Then let's not mention it again , she isn't even worth another thought , agreed ".

"Absolutely" he said "and now would you like some tea and toast?".

"Actually I could eat a horse , I haven't eaten since yesterday afternoon , remember?".

They got up , showered and dressed and Adam cooked a hearty breakfast of eggs ,bacon, sausages and tomatoes with loads of toast and coffee , compliments of his mother who had kindly offered to stock his fridge when she knew they were coming to stay for the weekend .

As they sorted out the dishes Adam pulled her towards him "Do you feel better now? Doughnut" She nodded and he could clearly see the deep affection written all over her face .

After another lingering kiss they could not resist one another and returned to the bedroom to make love again . This time slowly and sensually , repeatedly re-assuring one another of the everlasting love that they knew they would always have for each other . They just lay in each other's arms savouring every last moment of being together . Suddenly Adam looked at the clock , they had not realised the time and thought they had better get ready to go to visit his parents and Harry . They did not want to be late for lunch .

They arrived at mid-day and Harry was so thrilled to see them both . Vicky asked Diana if she could do anything to help.

"Don't worry , dear , it's all in hand" Diana smiled "James has got the photos from the cruise if you would like to see them , we forgot to bring them when we last saw you".

So Adam and Vicky sat with James in the lounge leisurely looking through all the lovely holiday snaps .

"Maybe I will take you on a cruise one day" Adam joked with Vicky .

"You already did and it was wonderful" she said referring to the trip on his boat that last Thursday of her holiday , the first time he had made love to her .

He looked so lovingly at her that it brought a lump to her throat and she almost cried . By the time they had finished looking at the photos , Diana came to tell them that the lunch was ready. They made their way through to the dining room and Harry insisted that he sit next to Vicky . Diana served melon as a starter and then a delicious pork roast followed by a super trifle for dessert, which was very tempting .

Whilst Diana and Vicky cleared away the dishes Adam took Harry over to his deckchair in the garden next door and sat with him for a while in the sunshine . Then Vicky came over and Adam stood so that she could sit in the deckchair beside Harry .

"There's a phone call for you" she told him , so Adam went back saying he would not be long .

"Is everything alright with you both?" enquired Harry .

"Yes" Vicky answered , although she knew he was not convinced , so she told him briefly what had happened the night before and how Celia had tried to come between them .

"Well I never" said Harry "how very sad"

"Please don't tell Adam that I said anything to you because it's all behind us now"

"Don't worry , I won't" promised Harry "The one thing I will say and always remember this , I know Adam like I know the back of my hand and he would never be unfaithful to you because I know how much he loves you . He is an honest , kind and gentle person who is totally genuine .

"Like you then Harry" she grinned . He looked at her with those twinkling eyes and smiled broadly .

At that moment Adam came back from next door . "That was Toby on the phone , he missed saying goodnight to us last night and rang to see if we had got home safely" he winked at Vicky and she knew he would fill her in on the rest later .

They noticed that Harry had fallen asleep so they left him there and Adam asked his mother if she minded if they went for a short walk on the beach .

"Of course not , you go and enjoy yourselves , we will see you both later" she smiled . Vicky really loved Diana , she was so very thoughtful .

They walked down the same path they had used on the night that Vicky had hurt her foot.

"Go very careful" Adam sounded worried , so he walked in front of her all the way , just in case she should stumble .

They reached the sand and she took off her shoes "At least it's light now and I can see if we encounter any jagged rocks" she laughed .

They found a delightful spot and sat down . The sun was warm and Adam gently pushed her down onto the sand and his lips came down on hers . She melted under the kiss and when it finished they both realised that they were crying .

"We could so easily have broken up yesterday and I can't bear to think about the consequences if we had" he murmured softly.

"We will try very hard not to think about it and be so glad that we are still together , that we have weathered the storm as they say". She pulled him down to her lips and this time she kissed him thoroughly . It made her feel warm and contented inside and she was just so relieved that the worst was over .

On the way back he told her that Toby and Celia had had a big fight the night before and that she had broken off the engagement and gone back to London that morning . Toby had known that the relationship had been deteriorating for some time now and he had been quite relieved when she had finished it .

"Well good riddance to bad rubbish then" Vicky said adamantly.

Adam held her hand tight as they walked up the cliff path . They peeked at Harry but he was still asleep , so they went back to the house .

Diana asked Vicky to come upstairs and look at the outfit she had bought for the wedding

The wedding that nearly never was , thought Vicky , feeling very relieved .

Diana's outfit was superb . An elegant suit which had a pale cream background with autumn gold , orange and brown flowers and a gold coloured hat with matching bag and shoes .

"Oh it's so lovely , you will look wonderful".

"I'm so glad you like it" she gave Vicky a big hug "You will never know how pleased we are about you and Adam getting married".

Vicky smiled back and thought , you will never know how glad I am either .

"Could I ask a big favour of you?"

"What is it?" Vicky asked frowning .

Diana went to the wardrobe and removed an ornate box . She opened it and brought out the most beautiful diamante tiara Vicky had ever seen .

"Would you honour me by wearing this on your wedding day , it's the one I wore when I married Adam's father and you will need something borrowed won't you?".

Vicky was speechless then gulped "The honour would be all mine" and she went over to Diana and hugged and kissed her.

Then they went through the old saying checking that Vicky had all she needed . Something old….Harry's locket , something new….her wedding dress , something borrowed ….Diana's tiara , something blue….her garter.

"I think we have thought of everything" smiled Vicky. So she and Diana went downstairs and Diana excitedly told James and Adam how thrilled she was about the heirloom being used at the wedding .

After a lovely tea of Ham salad and fresh fruit Vicky and Adam said their goodbyes and drove back to the apartment in Cowes .

"What shall we do tomorrow?" Vicky asked .

"Stay in bed all day and make mad passionate love together" laughed Adam in reply .

"Sounds good to me" she said looking lovingly at him and thanking her lucky stars that they were still together

Chapter 12.

THE next few weeks were spent getting Liz and Evie's dresses and head-dresses and arranging the flowers etc: Adam had arranged everything from the church , cars , men's suits to the reception venue on the island and of course he had sorted the honeymoon destination . He had booked 10 rooms for the Friday and Saturday in the hotel quite near to his parents house because some of the guests would be staying overnight . The hotel was a seventeenth century coaching Inn that nestled amongst thatched cottages in the old village right near the car park where Vicky had parked her car that first Sunday in May. Everything was arranged and the wedding was now only a few days away.

Early on the Friday morning , the day before the wedding , Grace and Robert were all packed and ready to go , so they rang Vicky before they left the house to say they were on their way to pick her up . She answered the phone and sounded quite nervous ."You okay, love?" asked her Dad.

"Just hoping nothing goes wrong at the last minute , Dad".

"Well we're just leaving so we will pick you up in about quarter of an hour", he rang off .

Vicky was all ready . Snowy was with her neighbour who was just looking after him for a couple of days until Jack and his family got back from the wedding .

Well this is it , she sighed , as she waited for her lift . She then sat on the sofa put her head back and closed her eyes and relaxed for a while thinking back to the day she had first met Adam and Harry and in no time at all her mum and dad had arrived and they helped her to load everything she needed into the car . She then locked up her little house and they set out to catch the ferry.

They arrived at the hotel in Shanklin about three and a half hours later .

Vicky and Adam had booked the bridal suite and it was fantastic . A king-size bed with a beautifully patterned antique headboard almost as wide as Vicky's lounge . Above the bed was a painting of a wedding scene , in which the bride and groom were just emerging from the church . The clothes they were wearing seemed to indicate that they were from the 1800's . The ceiling in the bedroom was inlaid with a blue and white Wedgwood design and the bay window in the room overlooked beautifully kept lawns and flower beds . The bathroom looked Victorian with a large cast iron bath on legs and a shower head that was as big as a dinner plate . After inspecting the suite with her mum and dad , she sat on the bed and did not know if the feeling she had in her stomach was excitement , nerves or hunger , so her dad ordered some tea and sandwiches to be sent up to the room .

After they had settled her in Grace and Robert went to their own room to un-pack . Grace had bought a very smart outfit in powder blue and had hired a matching hat from a shop in Devizes and Robert had the suit that Adam had hired for him .Their room was along the corridor near all the other guests . This left Vicky on her own for a while and as she ate her sandwich and drank her tea her thoughts once again went back to the visit she had made in May . Five months , she pondered , who would have credited all that had happened in such a short time . She was brought out of her reverie as the phone rang , she picked it up . "Hello".

"Hello my darling Doughnut".

She was so glad to hear Adam's voice . Although they had spoken on the phone they had not seen one another for over two weeks ."Oh Adam , I'm so glad it's you".

"Am I allowed to come up to our room today?".

"Of course , it's only bad luck if you see me tomorrow before I arrive at the church , I think . Anyway I'm not superstitious".

"I will be right up then".

Within three minutes they were in each others arms , hugging and kissing and almost crying , happy tears ,of course .

"Just think tomorrow you will be Mrs Adam Moore".

"I can't wait" she beamed as their lips met again .

"I have arranged a little get together this evening for all the guests staying here and my grandfather , my parents and Aunt Judith and Uncle Alvin are coming down , Is that alright?".

"I will look forward to that , especially meeting your Aunt Judith . Harry must be so excited that she and your uncle could come over for the wedding".

"He's ecstatic about everything to do with this wedding , I just hope he does not get too tired . I think everything is arranged now , I hope so anyway".

"Would you like a cup of tea , there's one in the pot".

He nodded , "Lovely , thanks".

So there they sat in the winged chairs either side of the old fashioned fireplace as if they were already married , drinking their tea . Vicky thoughts just fleetingly went back to Harry's story when Sarah imagined herself and Harry in the same position when they went out that day to the tea shop in Liverpool.

"Do you like the room?" Adam asked bringing her out of her trance .

"I love it" she smiled "but not as much as I love you".

The evening reception went very well and Vicky met some more of Adam's family and friends . She especially loved meeting Judith as she had heard so much about her .

Judith and Alvin had brought a silver dollar as a special present quoting the verse as they knew it . "Something old , something new , something borrowed , something blue and a silver dollar to wear in your shoe" Judith said as she handed the special coin to Vicky .

Vicky was thrilled as they wished her and Adam all the luck in the world .

Then all too soon it was time to say goodnight to everyone and Adam took Vicky up to her room , but he stayed on the thresh-hold and kissed her lovingly there . "See you in church tomorrow , Doughnut".

She nodded .

"Don't be late" he grinned .

She shook her head .

"I love you".

"I love you too" she replied ,and then he was gone .

Grace rang to say goodnight again and asked Vicky if she would be alright on her own .

"Quite alright , Mum, I will see you in the morning . I'm having breakfast in my room , so why don't you and Dad have yours sent up here as well .

"Okay , love , we will do that . Sleep tight . Love you".

The wedding ceremony was booked at the local church at 2 o'clock . The hairdresser was coming to the hotel at 10 am to do Vicky's hair and Liz , Grace and Evie's too . Could anything go wrong? She hoped not and surprisingly she fell asleep quite quickly thinking, tomorrow is my wedding day .

Everything went to plan in the morning and best of all the sun shone and they could not have wished for better weather .

When they were all dressed in their finery ,Vicky felt like a princess and Evie looked like one . Liz reminded Vicky to put the silver dollar in her shoe and the three of them looked a picture when her Dad came to the room to fetch them . The wedding car came for Liz and Evie first which left Vicky and her Dad alone for a while .

"You look absolutely gorgeous , love" he said with watery eyes . "He's a very fortunate man that Adam of yours , but I'm sure he knows that already".

"Thanks , Dad" she was almost crying herself ."We had better go downstairs now , I promised Adam that I wouldn't be late".

Her dad put his arm out to her and she hooked up her train and they made their way to the reception area where the car was waiting to take Vicky on the journey she had been dreaming of for all of her adult life .

Vicky arrived at the church and walked down the aisle on her father's arm at 2 o'clock . The organ was blasting out 'Here comes the Bride' and she seemed okay until Adam turned around and looked at her . Her legs just turned to jelly and her dad said "Steady now , my girl".

"I'm alright , Dad" she whispered although she still sounded nervous .

As she reached Adam he looked at her with such tenderness and whispered "You are so beautiful" and she knew he meant it . He would never know how much it meant to her either .

After they were married and all the photographs had been taken at the church , they all went to the Yacht Club for the reception . Vicky tried to put the memory of her last visit there into the back of her mind and neither she nor Adam mentioned it .

After a superb meal , the speeches , the cutting of the cake and everyone having a great party it was time for just the close family to go back to Adam's parents home .

When they had all arrived Adam took Harry across to his old garden . Although he was tired he insisted on going over to sit in his deckchair and talk to Sarah .

After a while Vicky suddenly missed Harry and decided to go over to see him . As she walked towards him in her wedding attire the smile on Harry's face was priceless " I have just been telling Sarah all about the wedding and how beautiful you look and how wonderful it is that you and Adam are married at last" he said with contentment .

"I want to thank you Harry because if I had not seen your magical old house from the café in the park I would never have met Adam again . Oh! Harry , this really has been the happiest day of my whole life" she held Harry's hand in hers and he squeezed it ."I am so excited about our future together and if our first child is a boy we're going to call him Harry".

Harry smiled at her and then closed his eyes .

As Vicky continued talking Harry's hand suddenly went limp . She froze with fear for a moment and could not speak . Just then Adam came to fetch his grandfather for his tea , but he saw Vicky's face and the tears running down her cheeks and he knew what had happened .

Vicky was still holding Harry's hand . "He was telling Sarah about the wedding" she sobbed softly.

"Well now he's gone to see her" he whispered as he bent down to embrace his precious grandfather . He tenderly picked up Harry's fragile body in his arms and gently carried him back to the house . Everyone was devastated but at least they knew Harry had died happily knowing that he had brought Adam and Vicky together .

Diana insisted that they still go on their honeymoon as that is what Harry would have wanted .

A week later , after the splendid honeymoon that was tinged with sadness was over , Adam and Vicky came back to attend Harry's funeral . He was laid to rest in the same plot as his beloved Sarah . Harry was 91 years old when he died and had had a wonderful life .

At the wake the solicitor called everyone into Harry's old sitting room for the reading of his last will and testament . Harry had left the old magical house to Vicky and Adam plus enough money to completely renovate it.

The solicitor then read a letter to the newly-weds written by Harry on the day he had given Vicky the gold locket . It read:

May 2007.

Dearest Adam and Vicky , my beloved grandson and his lovely wife .

I believe in fate , if I had not visited the cake shop in Liverpool , I would never have met your grandmother . Fate brought Vicky to the island and to the old house . I knew as soon as I saw you both together that you were made for each other just as my beloved Sarah and I were . I hope you have children , the thought of children , love and laughter in the house and garden again warms my heart

Be happy together forever .

With all our love from Sarah and Harry . xxx

As the solicitor finished reading the letter tears were falling from Vicky' chin and Adam held her tightly , trying hard himself to control emotions that were welling up inside of him.

Vicky knew then that she and her Adam were going to be in love forever just like Sarah and Harry had been before them . She also knew that they were going to love living in the magical house .

Epilogue.

THE renovations would start as soon as possible but to complete the whole house was going to take quite a long time . So meanwhile Adam and Vicky lived in Adam's house on the mainland until the old house was finished . Vicky eventually sold her fancy dress business and decided to work from home as a seamstress . They converted the little sitting room in the magical house , the one with the long window overlooking the sea , into a sewing room and every time she looked out into the garden she thought of dearest Harry sitting in his deckchair chatting to his beloved Sarah . They decided to re-name the house ' Sahara House' after Sarah and Harry .

On their first wedding anniversary they woke early and Adam had brought Vicky breakfast in bed . They exchanged cards and when Adam opened his there was a long poem , written by Vicky , inside .

The most precious day of my whole life
was when you married me
and I want to tell you , Darling, that
I'll love you 'til eternity .
It's a year ago today since the best day of my life
When you my own Prince Charming took me as your wife .
When I walked into the church that day,
down that long and narrow aisle
The most wonderful thing I saw looking at me,
was your wonderfully welcoming smile
No-one had ever shown me so much love before that day
I will never forget how special I felt ,
when you looked at me that way .
Thank you for telling me that day that I looked so beautiful
You will never know how that made
me feel , absolutely wonderful .
You touch the lives of all you meet and
your spirit is easy and free
How lucky I am to have you , Adam,
you really did choose me .
You have lovely brown eyes that dance
and your laughter is full of joy
Your smile is full of mischief and
your heart like a little boy .
You smell so good when you hold
me, I feel so safe and sound
You're kind , compassionate and caring , yes
in you all these virtues I've found .
I never mean to be cross with you ,
when things don't go quite right
You still find time to tell me you love me,
morning , noon and night .

You are genuinely forgiving , your heart is so sincere
I've loved every minute of us being together
in this our first special year.
I wouldn't be me without you , we are
just like strawberries and cream
I just hope that the rest of our wonderful
life will continue to be like a dream.
I need you like a babe needs it's mother,
you are my sunrise and sunset
I wouldn't change you for all the world ,
you're the best any woman could get .
No-one else could make me feel so complete ,
in my life's puzzle you're the final piece
Without you my world would be nothing,
without you my life would cease.
Home is where the heart is and my heart lies here with you
Thank you for working so very hard to
make sure all our dreams come true .
This has been the first year of our life,
at the moment built for two
But I know we will share many more ,
together we'll always come through .
Thank you for making me feel so good,
since the day I said 'I do'
You're cheeky and charming and wonderful
and Adam I will always love you .

Happy Anniversary , My Darling Adam.
All my everlasting love.
Vicky

x x x
PS . I'm pregnant!

By the time Adam had read it to the end they were both crying tears of joy . He sat on the bed and took her gently into his arms and kissed her. "That is the best present I could ever have" he said kissing her again .

When they had ended the kiss she told him that she had had the pregnancy confirmed and she and the baby were fine .

Adam and Vicky had two children , first a little boy named Harry Robert James , after Harry , of course and both their fathers . Then they had a little girl whom they named Sarah Daisy May , after Adam's grandmother , her favourite flower and the month that they had met .

As she stood in the garden one summers day shortly after Sarah was born Vicky , watching Adam with their two precious children , knew that she and Adam were now making their very own memories that would most certainly be made of love .

Lightning Source UK Ltd.
Milton Keynes UK
18 November 2009

146410UK00001B/7/P